Cassy gasped in amazement and stepped inside.

The room was filled with shelves and pedestals holding beautiful bronze sculptures. Animals, especially lions, seemed to be his specialty. They were exquisite.

She paused to crouch down before a pair of nearly life-size lions. "Absolutely incredible."

"Thank you."

Cassy rose with a shriek and whirled.

In the darkness just outside the room, deep-set eyes gleamed with a predator's assessment. Energy crackled as Gabriel Lowe took a sinuous step into the light.

Her gaze fastened on the scar that ran from the corner of his left eye to the edge of his strong jaw, adding gruesome detail to the fierce aura he projected. He was taller than she'd expected. Powerful shoulders tapered to a narrow waist. Lean hips and muscled thighs mesmerized her as he glided forward. Cassy forgot to breathe. Panic sent her gaze questing for an escape route.

There was nowhere to run. She was trapped.

Dear Reader,

If you like a tortured alpha hero, I've got one just for you. I've wanted to tell Gabriel Lowe's story for some time. In fact, the original opening was written more than ten years ago—some heroes need longer than others for their stories to come together. I hope you'll think Gabe was worth the wait. He's been hiding in the shadows of my mind a long time now. I'm happy to finally give him a voice.

Cassiopia started out naive and immature, but quickly showed me that a meek personality would hardly work for someone like Gabe. She rewrote her role to be a match for his surly disposition, and I found myself identifying with her as the story unfolded.

The plot itself came from the headlines several years ago when the anthrax scare hit the front pages and I thought, *What if?* While writing action and dialogue comes fairly easy to me, dealing with strong emotions does not. *Beautiful Beast* was a challenging story to tell. I hope you'll like the results.

Happy reading!

Dani Sinclair

DANI SINCLAIR

BEAUTIFUL BEAST

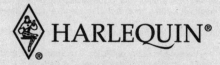

HARLEQUIN®

TORONTO • NEW YORK • LONDON
AMSTERDAM • PARIS • SYDNEY • HAMBURG
STOCKHOLM • ATHENS • TOKYO • MILAN • MADRID
PRAGUE • WARSAW • BUDAPEST • AUCKLAND

With thanks to Natashya Wilson for the concept, helpful corrections, suggestions, edits and hand-holding as required.

A heartfelt thank-you to Judy Fitzwater and Robyn Pope for plotting assistance, crunch-time reading, terrific suggestions and friendship above and beyond the call.

And for Roger, husband extraordinaire, who listened a lot, offered suggestions, ignored frustration and let me work when other things beckoned. You're the best!

Always, for Chip, Dan and Barb.

Love all you guys.

ISBN-13: 978-0-373-22935-2
ISBN-10:   0-373-22935-6

BEAUTIFUL BEAST

ABOUT THE AUTHOR

An avid reader, Dani Sinclair didn't start writing seriously until her two sons were grown. With the premier of *Mystery Baby* for Harlequin Intrigue in 1996, Dani's kept busy writing stories. Her third novel, *Better Watch Out*, was a RITA® Award finalist in 1998 while *The Specialist* was awarded Best Intrigue of the Year in 2000 by *Romantic Times BOOKclub*. Dani lives outside Washington, D.C., a place she's found to be a wonderful source for both intrigue and humor. You can write to her in care of the Harlequin Reader Service. Check out her Web page at www.danisinclair.com.

Books by Dani Sinclair

Don't miss any of our special offers. Write to us at the following address for information on our newest releases.

Harlequin Reader Service
U.S.: 3010 Walden Ave., P.O. Box 1325, Buffalo, NY 14269
Canadian: P.O. Box 609, Fort Erie, Ont. L2A 5X3

CAST OF CHARACTERS

Gabriel Lowe—The solitary soldier has no memory of what happened the day he was forever scarred and branded a liar and a murderer.

Cassiopia Richards—She's determined to clear her father's name and see that his murderer is brought to justice.

Beacher Coyle—He may be a silver-tongued ladies' man, but he's the only person Gabe trusts.

Major Frank Carstairs—He's always been Gabe's chief suspect in the theft of a deadly toxin. Too bad he died the day it was stolen.

Andrea Fielding—Dr. Pheng's lab assistant was Gabe's fiancée—even though her brother was antimilitary.

Major Bruce Huntington—He didn't like having Gabe under his command. Now he's certain Gabe will get what he deserves.

Rochelle Leeman—The gallery owner is beautiful, determined and bold enough to go after what she wants, no matter the consequences. And Gabe has what she wants.

Arthur Longstreet—The chief of security for Sunset Labs was new to the job when the toxin disappeared from under his nose.

Dr. Trung Pheng—The chief research chemist was working to create an antidote to the toxin when his work was stolen.

Dr. Powell Richards—His murder started the hunt for the missing toxin. Did the thieves turn on one of their own?

Len Sliffman—The former FBI man is trying to keep an open mind.

Prologue

Unease rode Gabe, but second lieutenants in the U.S. Army didn't question direct orders from a major, even one outside their direct chain of command. When Major Frank Carstairs gave an order, it was obeyed.

Besides, Gabe could hardly call his captain for verification. Everyone knew Captain Bruce Huntington didn't like Second Lieutenant Gabriel Lowe, who had been recently assigned to his military intelligence unit. And the order had nothing to do with Gabe's babysitting job. He was the newest person in the unit, and low man, so he got all the unwanted assignments.

The original orders had been to transport three vials of a deadly toxin from the military base in Frederick, Maryland, to Dr. Powell Richards at Sunburst Laboratory in Urbana, Maryland. Gabe was then to oversee security.

Everything had gone as planned. The doctor had accepted the toxin with no hitches yesterday, and today had been a normal day. The doctor had left early, and

Gabe had made certain the toxin was secured and his men in place before leaving. He'd been on his way home when Major Carstairs had ordered him to pick up Dr. Richards and escort the scientist to the base immediately.

Clearly something was wrong but no one, especially not the major, was going to bother explaining to him what that something was.

While the doctor had appeared stressed and preoccupied when he left for the day, Gabe didn't know him well enough to know if that was normal or not. Dr. Richards hadn't mentioned a problem and none of Gabe's men had reported anything since he left, so what was going on?

Parking the car on the narrow street, Gabe stared up at the Richards house as dusk laid claim to the neighborhood. There was no car in the driveway and no lights to indicate anyone was home.

Other houses sparkled with lights and life as dusk yielded quickly to the press of an early nightfall. A perfectly normal scene, yet Gabe felt something was off.

Uneasy, he stepped from his car trying to determine why his senses were crying an alert for no good reason. He felt oddly exposed. His hand itched for the comfort of his holstered service revolver.

He hesitated as headlights swept up the street. The garage door began to open. The approaching vehicle slowed to make the turn, giving Gabe a clear view of the driver. Dr. Richards appeared even more stressed and distracted than before. He didn't so much as glance at Gabe standing there. Something was definitely wrong.

Gabe's hand still hovered near his revolver as he

followed the car toward the house. He moved more quickly when it pulled all the way into the garage.

Without warning, a giant fireball rocked the neighborhood. Gabe reeled back. Something sliced his face as the garage exploded.

He ignored the warmth running down his cheek and sprinted for the car. A figure struggled to climb out as flames engulfed everything. A billowing wave of heat brought Gabe's hands up to cover his face.

The second, larger explosion sent Gabe sailing through the air. He landed with incredible force amid a hail of raining debris. His last coherent thought was that he should have listened to his instincts.

Chapter One

Frederick, Maryland
Present Day

A slender figure came around the far side of his house and sprinted across the front lawn to disappear in the hedge on the other side. Gabriel Lowe stopped walking. Not CID, FBI, Homeland Security or any of the other official types who watched his house from time to time. Their people would have approached his home in a much different fashion.

Female, based on the swing of nicely rounded hips in figure-hugging jeans. A long ponytail swished against a slender back covered by a fitted jacket. His intruder was obviously looking for a way inside. And in that instant, he knew who it had to be.

His fingers flexed and balled into fists. Jaw clenched, Gabe stepped off the sidewalk and slipped into the nearest shadow. He followed her silently, letting his anger build.

With a low-voiced, muttered imprecation, she battled her way behind the prickly juniper that squatted beneath his dining room window. Identity confirmed, Gabe faded back against the bole of the spreading oak tree a short distance from her.

Cassiopia Richards—the woman who had named him a murderer—gazed up at the window and sighed. She withdrew a ridiculously tiny pocketknife from her hip pocket and hesitated. The small blade was hard to see in the bit of moonlight that filtered between the high clouds, but her intention was clear.

Gabe was reluctant to accost her too soon. Would she actually go through with a criminal act?

She slit the screen and started to reach for the window itself. Abruptly, she stopped.

"Blast."

The utterance was a wisp of discord in the chilly night air. She struggled with the juniper branch that had clamped onto the back of her coat. Apparently, she didn't understand that an illegal activity like breaking and entering required silence and speed.

Not once did she bother to scan her surroundings. She wouldn't have seen him if she had, but she was either extremely sure of herself or totally inept. Watching her struggle with the bush, he was betting on the latter.

FRAZZLED, CASSY JERKED her coat free, half hoping this window would be locked like the others she had already tried. Then she could go home and come up with a new plan. This one was stupid. If she were caught...

She would not think about that. She couldn't afford to turn around and go home. If there was the slimmest chance Gabriel's friend Beacher Coyle had actually succeeded where everyone else had failed, she needed to do something.

She'd been a fool to listen to him in the first place. He'd almost convinced her that they were victims, like her father. He'd persuaded her to listen and now the golden-tongued son of a serpent wasn't answering his telephone. Gabriel had blown her off when she'd contacted him, and now Beacher was avoiding her calls. And if her suspicions were correct, Beacher had brought the results of his search to Gabriel.

They'd found the missing toxin and were going to sell it unless she stopped them. By the time she convinced someone in authority, it would be too late and she was not going to let them get away with it.

Not a sound disturbed the stillness of the night. Cassy had little fear of being observed, given the distance between the houses. The blasted neighborhood was dark enough to give her the creeps. Once more she adjusted the thin bits of plastic over her hands and reached up.

With a scraping, groaning racket all out of proportion to what she'd expected, the window yielded and slid to one side. Startled, she froze. Her heart thundered wildly in her chest. Her ponytail swung as she took a quick look around the yard and at the house next door.

GABE REMAINED MOTIONLESS as her eyes swept by him without faltering and continued on to the house next door. He could have told her she had nothing to worry about from that direction. The family inside would be glued to their television sets at this hour. Nothing less than an explosion would bring them to a door or window.

But what was Cassiopia Richards doing here in the first place? Perhaps he should have heard her out when she called the other day, but her patronizing tone had annoyed him. He'd never forgotten her tirade when he'd been trapped in that hospital bed. Gabe didn't owe her a thing.

She stared at the opening as if trying to screw up her courage to climb inside. Then she cast another nervous glance around. He waited.

THIS WAS NO TIME for paranoia, Cassy admonished herself. There was no one lurking nearby watching her every move, even if the back of her neck was crawling in warning. Gabriel Lowe was at his gym at this hour. While the sound of the window opening had been loud, it hadn't been loud enough to carry inside the house across the yard, and no one moved on the silent street. Not a single car had driven past since she got here.

Well, it wasn't every day she attempted to break into someone's home. Her nerves had a right to be jumpy. She was usually such a practical person.

Cassy gripped the windowsill and levered herself up. The jagged screen snagged on the elbow of her jacket. She yanked her arm back. The screen ripped free of the window and fell, tangling with the bush below. She froze in dismay and swore softly.

So much for hoping he wouldn't notice the torn screen.

ENTERTAINED DESPITE his annoyance, Gabe waited to see what she'd do next. What she did was seek a better grip, even though the weird, loose-fitting clear plastic covering her hands made the task harder than it should have been.

What were those things? They weren't the latex gloves that hugged the skin. These bits of clear plastic fit so loosely she seemed to be having trouble keeping them in place.

Cassiopia Richards had to be the most inept burglar ever. Her thrusting hand tangled in the sheer drape that covered the window. She tried to shove the material aside as she swung her leg up and over but the drape wasn't having any of it. In her attempt to avoid being wrapped in the filmy cloth, her leg apparently collided with the back of a chair.

Gabe nearly smiled. His dining room was small, the furniture too large for the space. He'd kept his parents' old stuff after he bought this place because the pieces served to fill the empty rooms. Since he was pretty much the only one who ever saw them, their relative size had never mattered, but her unexpected contact with the chair nearly reversed Cassiopia's direction. Even from where he stood he could hear the chair clatter against the table.

CASSY STOPPED MOVING half-in and half-out of the window. She stopped breathing as well. She waited for Gabriel Lowe to appear out of the darkness and condemn her. Even though she was almost positive he wasn't home, it seemed an inevitable thing to happen.

She cast another frantic glance around. The yard was pitch-black. She couldn't see a thing. There was no going back now. She expelled the breath of air and forced her other leg over the sill.

The drape swirled around her once more. She wriggled, colliding with the chair again. Cassy wrenched the gauzy fabric to one side in a frantic swipe. Off balance, she tumbled forward. Only pure dumb luck and the mahogany dining room table kept her from crashing to the floor.

Great. He'd never notice *that*. This was not an auspicious start to a life of crime. If she believed in omens, she'd turn around, climb back through that window and go home to bed. She could always get a decent lawyer in the morning.

She should have tried the authorities first. Maybe someone would have listened.

The prickly sensation that she was being watched would not go away. Her hand went to a side pocket and came out with the minuscule pocket flash. The attached key ring jingled as she moved.

If someone *had* been home, they'd have called the police by now. She'd made enough noise to wake the dead. Good thing she wasn't planning on a life of crime. Her nerves couldn't take much more of this.

Get it over with. Call out. See if someone *was* there.

GABE FLATTENED HIMSELF against the side of the house near the open window. He jumped when she spoke.

"Hello?"

Her scratchy voice was barely a whisper of sound.

"Is anybody home?"

And what would she do if he answered?

"Didn't think so, but I wanted to be sure."

Gabe shook his head. The woman was squirrel fodder. He'd been right to not waste time talking with her when she called.

The beam of her small flashlight swung away from the window. Gabe moved to where he could just see her vague outline. Her body radiated tension as she peered around the room. The resonant sound of the grandfather clock chiming the hour sent a tiny shriek past her lips.

"Idiot!"

On that, they were in complete agreement.

Muttering a profanity, she repositioned the chair at the table.

"No way am I going back out that window. When I leave tonight, I'm going out a door like any civilized burglar."

Thoroughly amused, Gabe watched as Cassiopia moved the small ray of light to search out a path to the kitchen. It would almost be a shame to ruin her evening by revealing his presence.

HER FRAZZLED NERVES were playing tricks on her. There was no one here. Gabriel Lowe *was* at the gym. Based on past observations she should have an hour and a half before he returned.

Cassy picked her way carefully through the maze of furniture. Fortunately for her, his tastes ran to the stark. While the heavy old pieces were oversized, he hadn't filled his home with bric-a-brac and clutter. And that seemed a little strange, given that he was supposed to be a sculptor. She'd expected to find dozens of ugly pieces scattered about.

Cassy shook her head. Who cared? The only thing that mattered was finding his home office, doing a quick search for what Beacher had found and getting away before either of them returned. She'd watched Gabriel enough to know that he spent most of his time in his basement. He even entertained Beacher down there, unless they sat around in the dark upstairs when he came to visit. Obviously, the basement was the place to start and she'd better hurry.

Finding a door next to the refrigerator, she reached for the handle. A mop stem hurled out of the darkness and cracked against her shoulder. Cassy leaped back, another small shriek escaping. Dislodged, a plastic pail rocked against the dustpan with a surprising clatter. The broom tipped over. She barely caught the handle in time to keep it from crashing to the floor.

HE WAS GOING TO HAVE to fix that wall mount for the mop and broom soon, Gabe thought, lips twitching. He'd waited until she'd stepped fully into the kitchen before slipping in through the open window without disturbing the drape or the chair. He'd cautiously taken a position near the hall entrance to the kitchen to see what she'd do next.

"I'm going to have a major heart attack before I even find the basement," she muttered so softly he had to strain to hear her. "Gabriel Lowe is going to come home and find my dead body on his kitchen floor wearing stupid baggie gloves. Why didn't I stop and pick up some latex ones?"

Stupid baggie gloves?

She replaced the mop, the broom and the pail and closed the door. The beam bobbled as she sent the anemic shaft of light toward the dining room entrance. He melted back before she shone it in the hall's direction, then moved to observe her when the light swung away again.

Taking a cautious step around the refrigerator, she continued moving until she reached the basement door.

She opened it gingerly and aimed the faint beam of light down the steps. He saw her shudder.

"This is *so* not a good idea."

Gabe agreed. What was she doing here? Didn't she realize his house was searched on a regular basis? The professionals could probably tell her the number of cans and the brand names of the soup in his kitchen cupboard on any given day. This had to have something to do with Beacher.

Gabe's humor dissolved as Cassiopia gripped the smooth wood banister and started down the stairs. He waited for her to reach the third step from the bottom. The board creaked loudly. Her gasp was swallowed by the darkness.

He took a step back from the opening. Sure enough, she sent that stupid little light back up before swinging it in front of her again. What she expected a beam of that size to reveal he wasn't sure. He probably hadn't even needed to move.

"Think of the squeak as an early warning system," she muttered.

That was exactly how he'd always looked at it. The narrow stairs were the only way in or out of the basement. He wondered if she knew that.

Using the flat of one hand and the weakening beam of light, she followed the curve of the wall to her right.

"If that man has a single rodent scurrying around down here I will come back and haunt him for all eternity."

He skimmed down the stairs noiselessly in her wake.

REALIZING SHE'D FOUND another room, Cassy swept her hand over the inside wall until she located the light switch. Waiting for her eyes to adjust to what seemed like sudden brilliance, she gaped in amazement and stepped inside.

The windowless space was filled with shelves and columned pedestals of varying heights. Each held a bronze sculpture or series of small sculptures. Animals, especially lions and big cats, seemed to be his specialty. He'd infused an almost living essence in each subject. They were exquisitely detailed.

Her hand reached out to stroke a deer poised in flight. She stopped before actually touching the lifelike bronze figurine and shook her head reverently. Slowly, she moved about the room in awe. Gabriel Lowe was an artist in the truest sense of the word. His talent was nothing short of amazing.

She paused to squat before a pair of identical, nearly life-sized bronzes. The crouching lions perched on elaborate, ebony wood bases on the tiled floor.

"Absolutely incredible."

"Thank you."

Cassy rose with a shriek and whirled.

Wreathed in the concealing darkness of the hall, deep-set eyes seemed to gleam with a predator's assessment as they surveyed her from beyond the room's pool of light. Panic sent her gaze questing for a nonexistent escape route.

Energy crackled as Gabriel Lowe took a sinuous step into the shaft of light.

Her gaze fastened on the twisted scar that ran from the corner of his left eye to the edge of his strong jaw. Horrible! It added gruesome detail to the sinister, fierce aura he projected.

He was broader and taller up close than she'd expected. Powerful shoulders tapered to a narrow waist. Lean hips and well-muscled thighs confirmed his fitness as he glided forward silently like some large, stalking cat.

Cassy forgot to breathe. The darkness seemed to thicken behind him, creating an impenetrable barrier. His fixed, implacable expression held her silent. Her heart drummed wildly against her rib cage.

There was nowhere to run even if she could have summoned the will to move. Like a cornered mouse, she knew she was trapped. The jig was up.

Gabriel Lowe was going to kill her, too.

Chapter Two

Gabe watched as Cassiopia's shocked gaze traveled the length of his scar before absorbing the rest of him. Well, his features hadn't been all that great even before the explosion. The bright red puckering of the scar had faded to white over time, but he knew its impact was still strong on unsuspecting people.

"Wha-what are you doing here?" she managed to gasp.

He arched his eyebrows pointedly and remained silent.

Cassiopia closed her eyes and groaned. "I knew I was going to get caught." She opened her eyes and grimaced. "I guess I should be glad you aren't a mad rapist."

He waited, keeping his expression blank, still reluctantly amused by her forced attempt at humor.

"You aren't, are you?"

"Which? Mad, or a rapist?"

"I know you aren't a rapist."

He raised his eyebrows. Color singed her cheeks but she pressed forward boldly.

"How mad are you?"

He came away from the door in a motion that brought him across the room in three long strides. Cassiopia took an inadvertent step back, stopping when her heel bumped the base of the nearest crouching lion.

"What makes you so sure I'm not a rapist?"

The silky tone of his words charged the air. Her lips parted without sound while her gaze fastened on his scar once more. She inhaled raggedly.

"Don't be absurd."

Her voice cracked, denying the false calm she was trying to project.

"Are you going to call the police?"

He let his expression darken, then crowded her deliberately, coming to a stop when he was inches from her face.

"Now why would I want to do that? The last thing a mad rapist wants is the police," he told her with silken menace.

Cassy refused to look away. "That isn't funny."

"Neither is breaking and entering."

She dropped her gaze. Gabe sensed it lingering on the scarred backs of his hands and made no effort to conceal the puckered skin. Let her look her fill. There were more scars than these, covered by his clothing.

A piece of burning siding had landed on him in the explosion nearly four years ago. He'd been unconscious, and only the fast action of a neighbor had kept him from burning to death. Any number of times he'd thought the man hadn't done him any favors.

Gabe was close enough to smell a bewitchingly light scent that wasn't some cloying perfume, but was utterly female. He tried to ignore that and focused on the play of color in her hair. Cassiopia Richards was…distracting.

Amazingly, there was neither pity nor horror in her

expression when she lifted her eyes. "You left me no choice," she told him with surprising fierceness. "You could have talked to me when I called you yesterday."

"I did."

Her lips thinned. "You told me to take a hike."

"I'm certain I was more polite than that."

"Stop playing games."

That stirred his anger once more. "I've said all I have to say on the subject of what happened four years ago. I'm not interested in repeating myself."

"Beacher claims you were an innocent victim, too."

Beacher was a fool. His friend was convinced Cassiopia knew something that would help them discover what Powell Richards had done with the missing toxin so he refused to give up his pursuit of her.

As Beacher had pointed out, *"That toxin's somewhere and we're going to find it and prove we had nothing to do with what happened."*

Gabe believed talking with Cassiopia was a waste of time. She'd been away at school when her father had taken the toxin from under Gabe's nose and gotten himself killed. And she'd scored an indelible impression on him that day in the hospital. She was too young, too passionate and obviously too impulsive to be of any help to them.

She summoned up a glare as if he'd spoken his thoughts aloud. "I'm leaving."

"You just got here."

Not many people could hold his gaze when he was in a temper. Given his overall size and his scars, he'd perfected the art of intimidation, but only the quickening leap of the pulse in her neck told him she wasn't as immune as she'd like him to believe.

Gabe stepped back. "Let's go."

"Where?"

"Upstairs."

The widening of those soft gray eyes brought a sudden vision of his bedroom and the two of them intertwined on twisted sheets. It had been a long time since he'd thought about sex and he banished the image instantly. But she seemed to be tuning in to his thoughts.

"I'm not going anywhere with you."

This time anxiety threaded her voice.

"You'd rather remain here?"

"Yes. Go ahead and call the police. I'd welcome them."

The bluster was gone. He'd finally succeeded in frightening her. It made him feel oddly ashamed.

"To the kitchen, Cassiopia," he told her more gently. "To talk. I may be mad—God knows I've been called worse—but I'm no rapist."

He stepped back even farther, giving her space. "Come or stay."

Her chin lifted in defiance. "I'll stay."

"Fine. But you should know that the way you entered is the only way out."

He crossed to the door and waited. She wasn't beautiful in the strictest sense of the word, but he'd definitely call her attractive. That rich brown hair with its hints of gold framed an oval face with high, prominent cheekbones and a long, graceful neck. Under other circumstances...

Who was he kidding? Under other circumstances she'd either take one look at his face and run the other way or cringe in pity. She faced him because she had no choice.

CASSY SOUGHT ANOTHER OPTION and realized there wasn't one. She was not going to cringe like a mouse even if this beast did have her well and truly trapped. She hated feeling afraid. She was in the wrong, but if he'd intended to kill her he'd have done it down here, not upstairs.

With a brief, accepting nod she squared her shoulders and marched over to him.

"Do not call me Cassiopia," she told him, pointing a plastic encased finger at his chest.

"Do you prefer Ms. Richards, or Dr. Richards?"

If he knew she was a Ph.D., he also knew she was a chemical engineer. She brushed aside Gabriel's question with a wave of her covered hand. "I go by Cassy."

He scowled, staring at her hand. "What *are* those things?"

Heat suffused her cheeks. Hastily, she pulled off the silly plastic shapes, feeling foolish.

"They come with packages of inexpensive hair dye."

"Brown isn't your natural color?"

"Of course it is! The hair dye belonged to my roommate."

"So you steal from others besides me."

"Betsy must have forgotten about it. And *I* didn't steal anything!"

He stilled so completely he could have been cast in bronze like the figurines around them. Shaken but refusing to give in to the alarm that charged every molecule of her body, Cassy forced herself to meet whatever retribution he demanded with her head high.

His stillness was so profound it was painful. Abruptly, he turned away.

"What are you going to do?" she demanded as another ripple of fear skated down her spine.

"Probably continue calling you Cassiopia. Cassy doesn't suit you at all."

He flicked off the light, plunging them into darkness.

"Hey!" Before panic could overwhelm her, light winked on at the end of the hall. There was nothing to do except follow, unless she wanted to stay in his basement all night.

The third step from the bottom made no sound for him, yet it squawked like a spitting cat the moment she set her foot on it. Was he even human?

Cassy shuddered. That horrible scar said he was all too human. He must have been an attractive man once. Actually, despite the scar, he wouldn't be bad-looking now if he'd stop scowling all the time. If nothing else, his aura of self-assured power commanded attention.

Cassy wanted to be glad he'd suffered for what he'd done, but Beacher had half convinced her otherwise. What if he were innocent? Could a man who could create such incredible beauty also destroy with such utter ruthlessness?

She'd been so enraged that day at the hospital she'd barely noticed Gabriel as a person. She'd needed a focus for her grief and rage and she'd taken it out on him, ignoring the fact that he'd been swaddled in bandages and attached to wires, tubes and monitors. Wrapped in her own emotions, she'd snuck inside his hospital room without a thought for anything except confronting the man responsible for her father's horrible death.

The memory of being pulled away while she ranted still shamed her. Even then his gaze had been dark and troubling. She'd had plenty of time to think about things since then. Letting go of her anger had been hard, but Beacher had pressed her to listen to him until he finally persuaded her to see that they might have been victims, too.

Gabriel hadn't hurt her just now, and he hadn't called the police. Of course he might be planning to call when they got upstairs, but either he and Beacher were guilty of murder and treason, or they'd been framed, as she was sure her father had been framed.

Had Beacher been playing both of them? Was he even now on his way out of the country with the deadly toxin?

Gabriel flipped on the kitchen light and shrugged out of his black cloth jacket, draping it neatly over the back of one of the two chairs at the tiny kitchen table. The black turtleneck hugged his shoulders and well-defined torso. He was lean and fit and scary in every way.

She'd made it a point to learn as much as she could about both men after Beacher began pestering her. Gabriel seldom left the small house he'd purchased after leaving the military on disability. He never socialized. Beacher was his only real friend as far as she could determine. The two had worked together at the army base, though their friendship dated back several years to when they were neighbors growing up. Gabriel had gone to a military academy. Beacher had gone to college and then joined a private security company. They both ended up working at the same military base and immediately resumed their friendship.

"Sit," Gabriel ordered without turning around. He crossed to the sink and began washing his hands.

"Am I supposed to bark now and wag my tail?"

He slanted her a startled glance. Unexpected humor lightened his dark-eyed stare.

"Skip the bark." And he turned back to the sink.

Outraged, Cassy wished she dared to toss something at him, but the room was immaculately clean. Even if she'd really wanted to, there wasn't a single loose object on the white countertop or the tiny kitchen table. Pale yellow walls and white cabinets did what they could to lighten the space, but it was so small there was barely room to turn around. Cassy would have guessed the kitchen was never used until he dried his hands and began opening cupboards.

Like the rest of the house, the cupboards were neat and orderly and filled with the sort of stuff she saw in her married friends' kitchens. The man even had a rack of spices. She thought of her own empty cupboards and shook her head. She never cooked if she could avoid it.

Gabriel set an electric kettle to boil. With fluid, economical motions that would have suited a laboratory, he removed two large brown mugs and a pair of small, matching plates. An odd-looking teapot in the shape of a dragon joined the rest on the pristine counter.

"What are you doing?"

He didn't spare her a glance. "Brewing tea."

"Tea?"

She'd broken into his house and he was making her tea? What was going on here? Was he stalling for some reason?

"You don't like tea?"

"Mostly I drink it iced."

He made a face and pulled a small cheesecake from a well-stocked refrigerator. Slicing two perfect wedges, he transferred them to the plates without a wasted motion.

"Sit down, Cassiopia."

She gritted her teeth. "I'd rather stand."

His granite face bore no expression as he turned. Hooded eyes focused on her with an unblinking stare that was totally unnerving. Set against the harsh planes of his face, she decided they weren't the tawny eyes of a lion but dark ebony wells of silent turbulence. Gabriel had seen too much of the unpleasant side of life. The impression of barely leashed power lent him a quiet menace that made her tremble. No one looked less like a sculptor.

Cassy knew sculpting had been part of his physical therapy after he was injured, but did he realize what a talent he had? She was pretty sure most people studied for years before they could create the sort of breathtaking beauty he'd captured in the pieces downstairs.

"Do you want to talk or not?" he asked in that deceptively soft voice.

Not. When he gazed at her like that she wanted to run far and fast. Too bad that wasn't an option.

"Yes."

He looked from her to the table without another word.

Cassy conceded defeat. She pulled out the chair that didn't hold his jacket and sat down, glad for the warmth of her own lightweight jacket even though the house itself wasn't cold.

Immediately, he turned back to the counter and measured tea leaves as if scientific precision was called for. Steam drifted from the spout of the dragon, shaped to be its mouth.

Great. Even his teapot breathed smoke. She might be better off if he simply called the police.

Opening a drawer, he withdrew two plain blue place mats and set them on the table. He added forks, spoons and cloth napkins without a word.

His black turtleneck and dark jeans were spotted by stains of what appeared to be mud. However, his hands, including his fingernails, were scrupulously clean. Cassy noticed that his fingers and palms weren't burnt like the backs of his hands.

"Lemon?"

Cassiopia jumped. "What?"

"Would you like lemon with your tea?"

Gabe pronounced each word with deliberate care. She raised her chin.

"No, thank you. Just sugar."

He withdrew a glass sugar bowl from another cupboard and set it on the table.

"Have you had time to come up with a plausible explanation yet?"

She inhaled sharply. Obviously, she hadn't.

"You weren't supposed to be home."

"Oh?"

"You usually go to your gym at this hour."

"Should I feel flattered that you've been spying on me?"

Gabe set a slice of cheesecake and a cup in front of

her and settled in the opposite chair. Instantly, the small room seemed to shrink even further. This had been a bad idea. He did not want to find her attractive.

"Your bad luck," he continued. "I took a walk tonight, instead."

"Isn't it just?"

Her blush told him she hadn't meant to say that out loud.

"What did you expect to find in my basement?"

"Not those incredible sculptures."

She was stalling.

"I didn't realize you were so gifted." The color in her cheeks deepened. She ducked her head and picked up her fork without looking at him.

"Gifted?"

That jerked her face up. "You're extremely talented and you know it."

He inclined his head in acceptance.

CASSY WATCHED HIM fork up a bite of cheesecake. He slid the morsel from his fork to his mouth and chewed with pleasure. She had never realized how sexy eating could be.

She quickly banished the inappropriate thought. There was nothing sexy about Gabriel Lowe. Okay, there was, but he was more dangerous than he was appealing and she'd do well to keep that in mind. Except, surely she didn't have to be intimidated by a man who could create such sensitive works of art.

"Your sculptures look like something in a museum," she told him honestly. "You shouldn't be hiding them away in your basement."

Too late, she clamped her lips shut. What was she doing, lecturing the man?

"I'm flattered." He poured them both a cup of tea without expression.

Gabriel might not be crouching like the lifelike set of lions on his floor downstairs, but the resemblance was still uncanny. Like his metal counterparts, he, too, seemed to be waiting to pounce. Yet she couldn't dismiss the idea that he was silently laughing at her.

"Why are you here, Cassiopia?"

She swallowed hastily. "I want what Beacher Coyle gave you."

He stilled. Though the kitchen lights were on, an ominous darkness seemed to fill the room.

"Is that right?"

The mildness of his tone was a clear rattle of warning. She hoped her quaking was all on the inside.

"We're engaged to be married."

A mistake. She knew it the moment the blurted words were past her lips. She'd never been any good at lying. Why hadn't she thought ahead, prepared something to tell him?

His glance went to where her left hand lay clenched at the edge of the table. "He never mentioned a fiancée."

She wanted to look away but couldn't. Her gaze riveted on that terrible scar. Gabriel and Beacher were close friends. Of course he knew she was lying, but she had no choice now but to keep going or admit the truth.

"We haven't made a formal announcement yet."

If only she'd had a few minutes to come up with something better than a phony engagement.

"He hasn't bought you a ring yet, either."

Her mouth went dry. "No."

"Do you know the password?"

Cold, then heat, flooded her. Was he serious? He looked serious.

"You're making that up!"

She was certain he'd made it up, but his expression never altered. Gabriel waited. Unnerved, she tried to think of something plausible to say and failed.

"Why would he tell you to sneak in through a window?"

"He didn't. But I could hardly call you again and ask for an invitation, now could I?"

Dropping her fork to the plate with a clatter, she glared at him, defying him to contradict her. "You would have hung up on me again."

Was that the faintest trace of a curve to his lips?

"Actually, I wouldn't have answered your call at all," he told her, unperturbed.

He reached for his tea cup and took a swallow. "Why didn't Beacher come himself?"

Danger. This lion was waiting to pounce and tear her to shreds. She took a breath to steady her nerves.

"He couldn't."

"Why?"

Her heart raced. He was toying with her, she was almost certain of it. "I think he's in some sort of trouble."

"You think."

She held his gaze. "Just give me what he gave you."

"Let's both go to see him."

"No!"

"No?"

His misleadingly docile tone sent every nerve in her body clanging in alarm. She'd made a hash of everything.

Gabriel leaned back in his chair with an inscrutable expression, but she knew she'd lost. If Beacher had found the toxin and given it to him he wasn't going to tell her.

He bared his teeth. It was not a humorous smile.

"Want to try again?"

"You don't believe me!"

His mocking expression was confirmation.

Defeat lay like bitter ashes in her mouth. Everyone seemed to agree that her father had taken the toxin and all the research from the lab itself, even though he had no motive. The working theory was that he'd conspired with Gabriel, and possibly Beacher, to steal the toxin and sell it to the highest bidder.

The authorities further decided that Gabriel had double-crossed her father and set charges to kill him and destroy any evidence. They believed her father had come home unexpectedly and set off the explosions before Gabriel could get away. There was no other explanation as to why Gabriel had been at the house that day. As far as she knew, he'd never even offered one.

She wasn't sure where Beacher fit into this scenario, but there were a lot of things no one was telling her. She only knew the consensus was that the three men had conspired to steal the missing toxin and all the research that accompanied it. She assumed the authorities believed Gabriel and Beacher were simply waiting for the furor to die down to sell what they'd stolen. But it never had. The investigation had stayed as active as if the theft had happened yesterday. She couldn't count the number of times she'd been questioned.

"Beacher didn't send you, did he?" Gabriel asked.

"Of course he did." She tried to sound forceful. He might feel sure she was lying, but until he spoke to Beacher he couldn't be positive.

He took another bite of cheesecake and leaned back. She would not squirm under that intense stare no matter how much she wanted to. Instead, she focused on a small scar on his neck that his turtleneck didn't completely cover.

Was he scarred all over? Was that why his fiancée had broken their engagement while he was still in the hospital? Cassy had never spoken with Andrea Fielding, but she'd seen the beautiful lab assistant with Dr. Pheng. Dr. Pheng had sent the toxin to her father in the first place, which wasn't surprising. They were the top men in their field, friends as well as rivals since they had been graduate students together.

Cassy knew Dr. Pheng and Andrea Fielding had come under tight scrutiny as well. Everyone remotely connected to the toxin had, but only her father and Gabriel had had the opportunity to steal it.

With a sigh, she set down her fork. "Are you going to have me arrested?"

"Arrested?" He seemed to savor the word. "I don't think there's any need to have you arrested over some minor damage."

She ignored the heat in her cheeks once more. "I'll send you a check for the drapes."

"And the screen?" he asked blandly.

"Yes, blast it. The screen, too."

"I think we can come up with a more suitable punishment to fit this crime, don't you?"

Cassy moistened suddenly dry lips. She was completely alone in a house with a man everyone believed was a criminal and worse. And she'd let down her guard!

"I'd rather be arrested."

"Do I make you nervous, Cassiopia?"

Did lambs sleep with lions? Of course he made her nervous. If her palms grew any damper she'd drip all over the table, but she'd never give him the satisfaction of admitting as much.

"I'm not afraid of you."

His dark expression lightened. If he smiled at her now she'd toss her cheesecake at him.

"Good," he said neutrally and took another sip of tea.

She released the breath she'd been holding. "I'm going to leave."

"Without what you came for?"

"Are you going to give it to me?"

"No."

So Beacher had given him something! Or was he toying with her again?

"This is a waste of time."

"Not precisely. I rarely have visitors. Try the tea. It's a special blend."

He was definitely toying with her. "To think I was going to apologize. I can see it would have been a waste of breath."

The eyebrows arched once more. "For breaking into my house?"

"No! For that day at the hospital."

Humor vanished in an instant. His jaw hardened.

"Does that mean you no longer believe I murdered your father?"

Cassy wasn't sure what she believed anymore. The authorities claimed Gabriel had had no opportunity to remove the toxin from the lab alone. Only her father could have done so, and *that* she would never accept.

Her father had been understandably devastated by the sudden death of his wife only two weeks earlier. So was she, but no amount of grief would have caused her father to compromise his job.

"Did you kill him?" He wouldn't tell her the truth if he had, but she had to ask.

"No."

She waited until it became obvious he wasn't going to elaborate. "That's all you're going to say? Just 'no'?"

"I said all I had to say four years ago," he told her with deceptive mildness. "Finish your cheesecake."

Cassy shoved her plate aside. "I am finished."

His eyes narrowed. He set down his fork with careful deliberation. "Then it's time for you to leave."

"You're going to throw me out?"

"If you won't go under your own power."

He'd do it, too. She'd successfully roused the beast. Every instinct told her to get up and go, but she couldn't. She hadn't accomplished anything.

"I want what Beacher gave you."

"We don't always get what we want, Cassiopia."

For a millisecond, it was as if she had a clear window into his troubled soul. A lonely beast prowled there. Cassy couldn't help but feel sorry for him.

He stood in a fluid motion that caught her unprepared.

"When you see him, tell your *fiancé* I want to talk with him."

She could have refused to move. She wanted to refuse, but her legs were already drawing her to her feet. The menace in the room was too thick to ignore.

"You're a real bastard."

"Is it my turn to call you a name now?"

He didn't smile.

"Goodbye, Cassiopia. Don't come here again."

Seeing no choice, she walked down the hall toward the front door, aware of him at her back close enough to touch. Desperately, she tried to think of something else she could do or say to change the situation, but nothing came to mind.

He opened the door without a word and waited.

"If even one of those vials is opened a lot of innocent people will die. I wonder if even you could live with that."

Rage flashed across his expression. Cassy stepped onto the stoop, words of apology forming on her lips, but he closed the door in her face.

A chill breeze brushed her skin. Cassy shivered. She couldn't help thinking Gabriel Lowe was innocent after all.

Chapter Three

Anger would get him nowhere. Gabe snagged his coat, pulling it on as he left by the kitchen door. Swiftly, he moved around the side of the house only to find he needn't have hurried. Cassiopia trudged down the sidewalk slowly, her posture showing her dejection.

Unless that, too, was part of her act.

He didn't have time for this. His first commission was waiting on the worktable downstairs. If he wanted it completed on time, he had to finish shaping the clay tonight.

He knew little about Cassiopia Richards beyond the fact that she had a quick temper, made a laughable burglar and was a poor liar. If she and Beacher were engaged he'd eat all his works in progress.

How had she known Beacher had given him anything?

The minute his friend had showed up last night Gabe had known there was trouble, but Beacher had put him off. He'd handed Gabe a small package and asked him to hold it without questions until he returned.

"Don't open it, okay? I'll explain tomorrow when I come back." His expression had been grim. *"I don't*

have time to explain right now. There's someone I have to meet and I'm running late."

He wouldn't say who or what was in the package and, as of yet, he hadn't returned with explanations. How had Cassiopia known?

Beacher knew Gabe's house was searched on a regular basis. He wouldn't have asked Gabe to hold something that would get them both tossed in prison. Not when, at the cost of his own reputation, Beacher had stood by Gabe when no one else would. There was no one Gabe trusted the way he trusted Beacher so he hadn't pressed for answers. He regretted that now.

Something was wrong. Beacher should have shown by now. He'd give his friend until morning, then he was going to see what Beacher felt needed to be hidden from the irritating woman.

She stopped beside a small coupe and looked back at the house. Gabe stilled, willing her to see him as just another shadow once more.

Slapping the roof of her car in frustration, she climbed inside and started the engine. As she pulled away from the curb he made a mental note of the license plate and hurried to his backyard, bypassing his truck. The motorcycle started with its usual roar. He picked her up a few minutes later, traveling at a sedate rate of speed on the city streets.

Gabe hung well back. If she knew about his habit of going to the gym in the evening, she knew he rode a motorcycle. Following her was probably a waste of precious time. He'd take bets she was on her way home and not on her way to meet Beacher, but he had to be sure.

It was a bet he would have won.

When she turned into the parking lot of a row of modest town houses, he pulled over on the main road and waited. She took her time exiting the car. He used that time to survey the area.

Something moved furtively between two parked cars. Cassiopia had climbed out and was heading in that same direction, a large cloth handbag she hadn't had earlier slung over one shoulder.

Instincts screaming, Gabe kicked the bike to life. He roared into the lot as the crouching figure leaped from between the cars and rushed her. Cassiopia went down. The pair struggled briefly before the hooded figure took off, disappearing around the corner of the building with her bag.

Gabe sent the bike onto the sidewalk in pursuit. Grass and dirt spun under his wheels as he tore after the fleeing figure, only to come to an abrupt halt at a privacy fence blocking his path.

Spotting a gate, he leaped off the bike. The gate was locked or jammed, but the attacker hadn't had time to go anywhere else. Gabe scaled the wood fence. Abruptly, light flooded the small enclosure on the other side. A shape appeared in the sliding glass door holding a gun.

"Police officer! Hold it right there."

Gabe swore under his breath. From his perch on top of the swaying section of fence he saw something moving in the enclosure next door.

"A woman out front was just accosted," he told the cop. "I chased the suspect back here. He's in the yard next door."

"Get down. Slowly."

This cop already had his suspect. Gabe was dressed

in black and wearing a helmet. Until the cop knew for sure what was going on, he wasn't going to listen to anything Gabe said. Jaw clenched, he dropped to the ground, careful to keep his hands in plain sight.

"Flat on the ground," the man ordered. "Hands above your head."

With a sigh, Gabe obeyed. His helmet made the position more uncomfortable than it would have been otherwise.

"Could you at least have someone make sure Cassiopia's okay? I think she was only knocked to the ground, but I saw a knife when he took her purse."

"You know Cassy?" he asked suspiciously.

Not nearly as well as he was going to know her.

"She was just attacked out front."

He suffered through the pat-down and rose slowly when the officer told him to get up. By then they could both hear the approaching siren. The attacker had had plenty of time to disappear.

"Okay to remove my helmet?"

"No."

This man was no rookie. A helmet could be thrown.

Minutes later Gabe was relieved to see Cassiopia standing out front with a pair of neighbors. She appeared shaken, but unhurt. A marked police cruiser, lights flashing, pulled up. The female officer exchanged greetings with the man at his back.

"You can take it off now," the cop told him.

Gabe removed the helmet slowly and waited. They didn't seem to notice Cassiopia's shocked surprise at seeing him. The cop at his back spoke before she could say anything that would have landed him in handcuffs.

"Cassy, do you know this guy?"

Instead of denouncing him, she nodded.

"Gabriel Lowe. He went after the man who grabbed my purse."

Gabe sensed the officer putting away his weapon.

"You can lower your hands now."

Faces continued to appear in windows as a second cruiser joined the first. A small crowd gathered to listen while Cassiopia explained what had happened. Then it was Gabe's turn. The cops eyed his scar and treated him with wary respect as he explained his assumption that the person had gone in through the nearest gate and jumped the fence into the next yard.

"I only saw you," her neighbor stated.

A third unit pulled into the parking area.

"He's probably long gone, but we'd better do a sweep," the female officer suggested.

Eventually, Gabe was allowed to retrieve his bike from the side yard. As he walked it back to the parking lot Cassiopia strode over to him.

"You followed me home!"

"No need for thanks."

"Thank *you?*" She bristled.

"You're welcome. And you might want to lower your voice unless you want to explain to the cops how we know each other."

"You wouldn't dare!"

Gabe waited.

She fumed, but lowered her voice. "Why did you follow me?"

"To see where you were going. Do you know who attacked you?"

"Of course not! You heard me tell the police he was wearing a hooded sweatshirt with a scarf over his face."

There was no use pointing out that the one didn't negate the other.

"Is your roommate home?"

"I don't have a roommate." She blinked in sudden comprehension. "Oh. The hair dye. Betsy moved out last month. She got married."

He scowled. He didn't like thinking about Cassiopia alone and vulnerable inside that town house.

"You might want to stay somewhere else tonight."

"Why? He already got my purse. The house is safe. My keys were in my hand so he didn't get them. It all happened so fast I didn't have time to go for his eyes with them."

She would have done it, too.

"You believe it was a simple purse snatching?"

"Of cour—"

Her eyes turned to saucers. Her voice dropped even lower.

"No one knew I was going to your place tonight."

"Not even Beacher?"

"You think that was Beacher?"

Though obviously shocked by the idea, her words were barely above a whisper.

"No." Gabe shook his head decisively. "Too thin. Most likely a teenager or a woman."

"A woman!"

Gabe shrugged. "Who else knew your plan tonight?"

"No one."

Unfortunately, he believed her. "Then someone is watching you, too."

A flash of fear.

"What do you mean? Why do you assume this wasn't—?"

"Ms. Richards?"

CASSY SPUN TO FACE the approaching officer. In the woman's hand was her large cloth purse. The cut strap dangled limply.

"You found it!"

"This is yours, then?"

"Yes!"

Thank God. Gabriel had been wrong after all. It had been nothing more than a simple purse snatching.

"It was on the ground behind one of the units out back. You want to check to see what's missing?"

The bag was already open. She dug around inside a second before looking up.

"My wallet's gone." No surprise there.

"How much money did you have?"

"A twenty, two fives and seven ones." She knew the exact amount down to the sixty-seven cents in change.

"Credit cards?"

Cassiopia rattled off the name of her cards while the officer wrote the information in a small notebook.

"Driver's license?"

"No. Fortunately, I keep that in a separate folder with my health insurance card. They're still here."

The officer nodded. "You'd better notify your credit card companies right away."

"Yes. Was there any sign of the person who took it?"

"No, ma'am. I'm sorry."

So was she. Had they caught the person, Cassy

would have felt better. Gabriel's suspicions had made her jittery. When the officer finally had all the information from her and left, Cassy turned back to Gabe.

"See? Just a purse snatching."

His expression didn't change. "Maybe."

"You're trying to scare me."

"You aren't stupid."

"I'm not paranoid, either."

His lips twisted wryly, but he gazed at her with a dark frown. "You can come back to my place if you want."

The grudging offer widened her eyes. "Why?"

He remained silent.

"You don't think it was a purse snatching. You think he'll come back." What if Gabriel were right? "But I don't have anything."

"He doesn't know that."

Shaken, she shook her head. "You're in more danger than I am. You're the one holding whatever Beacher gave you."

GABE COULD SEE it was pointless to press her. He'd warned her. That was all he could do.

"I can't go with you," she insisted.

He replaced his helmet.

"I'm not afraid."

His jaw tightened. "You should be."

She stepped back on the curb as he kicked the bike to life. Cursing Beacher and everyone remotely connected to the missing toxin, Gabe turned for home.

Probably, she'd be fine. Tonight's attack could have been exactly what it appeared to be, a kid out to rob whomever fate placed in front of him.

On the other hand, it could have been something else entirely. He hoped he was wrong. He also hoped a little of his paranoia would rub off on Cassiopia. It would be a shame for all that feminine fire to end up extinguished on a morgue slab somewhere.

He didn't doubt for a moment that this was connected to what Beacher had given him to hold. His friend had some major explaining to do.

Halfway home he detoured to Beacher's apartment. He'd only been there a handful of times, but he knew which unit was his friend's. No lights showed and there was no familiar car in the parking lot.

Gabe used his cell phone and called Beacher's number anyway. The answering machine picked up on the fourth ring. Next he tried Beacher's cell phone and was immediately sent to voice mail. Gabe left pithy messages on both and text messaged his friend for good measure. There was nothing more he could do now except worry. He'd had years to perfect that ability.

As he neatened his kitchen several minutes later he debated getting the package and opening it without waiting. The size and shape were about right to hold a hard drive and a few other things, but if Beacher had found the missing toxin after all these years, surely he would have told Gabe. Either he trusted his friend or he didn't.

Gabe went down to the basement and hesitated only a second before turning away from his display room to his workroom on the other side of the stairs. He trusted Beacher. He would wait.

The nearly completed piece he'd been commissioned to do sat on one of several worktables under a cloth.

Working with his hands generally freed Gabe's mind for thinking, but he had to force his thoughts to concentrate on the rose bush and not Beacher.

The bush was proving to be a real challenge. The pair of chipmunks beneath the bush were finished to his satisfaction. So was the general shape of the bush, but Gabe had never tackled individual leaves and roses this small before.

As his fingers stroked a small petal to life his thoughts returned to Cassiopia. Not a day had gone by that he and Beacher hadn't tried to learn the truth of what had happened four years ago. Together and independently they had spoken to, or tried to speak with, everyone connected with the toxin. Beacher had always felt Cassiopia might know something useful, but it had been only recently that she'd agreed to talk with him.

Beacher was nothing if not persistent and knowing him, Gabe suspected his friend had begun to date her in an effort to get her to open up. She was an attractive woman and Beacher liked attractive women—but not enough to get himself engaged to one.

Cassiopia was definitely attractive. Slimmer now than he remembered, her features were more refined, but she hadn't lost any of that temper even if she did have it under better control.

A tiny rose blossomed to full beauty beneath his stiff fingers. Pleased, he moistened his hands and worked another.

Even if they were dating, Cassiopia should have known better than to make such a ridiculous claim. Beacher engaged? Never happen. Not even to someone as interesting as her. Beacher's little black book was filled with beautiful, interesting women. He had more listings than some telephone directories.

Gabe tackled a series of delicate leaves, marking each vein with careful precision.

How had she known Beacher had given him that package unless Beacher had told her? She'd made no secret of the fact that she'd been watching Gabe. Had she also been following Beacher?

Gabe was so used to being watched and followed he barely paid any attention anymore. Open surveillance was part of the government's harassment tactics so Gabe ignored them. That was probably why he'd never noticed her.

His finger flew as he mulled that over.

Cassiopia had implied the package contained the missing vials of toxin. Did she really believe that?

Did he?

Only desperation would have sent her into his home tonight. Surely she knew he was still being monitored by all the forces Homeland Security, the FBI and the United States Army could bring to bear on him.

Was it possible?

He screwed up a leaf in a moment of frustration and had to start again.

He would not give in to paranoia. Beacher would explain everything when he showed up. And he *would* show up. Eventually. For now, Gabe needed to keep his mind on his work.

The bush was coming together better than he'd anticipated. Rochelle Leeman would be pleased. He only hoped his creation wouldn't prove too intricate for Denny and the Bailin Brothers to mold and cast.

Gabe had been fortunate to stumble on Denny Foster when he'd gone looking for someone to teach him how to turn his sculptures into finished bronze pieces. The garrulous moldmaker had been a font of knowledge and connections.

Gabe still wasn't sure how he'd let the old man talk him into showing his work to Rochelle. Even more puzzling was how the stunning gallery owner had managed to convince him his work would not only sell, but sell for big bucks.

The trill of the telephone startled Gabe from his working concentration. The clock on the wall told him it was already 1:40 a.m.

Beacher! Finally.

He wiped his hands while checking the caller ID. A cell phone number, but not Beacher's. Gabe answered anyway.

"Lowe."

"Go ahead and say I told you so," Cassiopia began without preamble.

His stomach gave a lurch at the sound of her stressed voice. "You okay?"

"Yes. I'm outside your front door. Is your offer of a safe haven still open?"

"I'll be right up."

He disconnected and retrieved his gun from its hiding place under a nearby workbench before taking the stairs in twos. Not bothering with lights, he went to the window to check the street before going to the door. Cassiopia's car wasn't in sight and there were no unfamiliar vehicles parked along the street. Neither of those meant a thing, but only one figure was visible on his stoop. He opened the door cautiously, weapon ready.

Cassiopia stared from the gun to him.

"If you plan to shoot me, forget it. I'll go to a motel. I probably should have done that anyhow."

He yanked her inside. "You're alone?"

"No, the marching band is down the street."

"Where's your car?"

"I parked on the next street over. I didn't want anyone to see it in front of your house."

He couldn't decide if she was playing him. "Were you followed?"

"Of course not! I was watching for that."

Given her earlier performance, she wouldn't have the ability to spot a professional tail.

"Stay here."

She gripped his arm. "Where are you going?"

He gave her a hard look. She dropped her hand and followed him down the dark hall to the kitchen.

"Wait," he commanded, heading for the door.

"Sit. Stay. We're really going to have to work on your people skills."

Wanting to smile despite the situation, Gabe slipped out the back door. A thorough search of the neighborhood turned up two prowling cats, one brazen raccoon and a deer munching a neighbor's azalea bush. Cassiopia's car was exactly where she'd said it would be. There were no signs that anyone human lurked nearby.

Returning to the house, Gabe found her still standing in his kitchen muttering under her breath. Once again, she eyed the gun in his hand.

"You took long enough. I kept waiting for shots."

If it hadn't been for the slight tremor in the hand she used to pull back a thread of hair, he'd have thought her annoyed but calm. She wasn't calm. He slid the weapon into his waistband.

"Relax and tell me what happened."

"The two are mutually exclusive."

"Try."

She made a face, then sighed. "I couldn't sleep. It was your fault. I kept thinking about what you said. You know, that maybe someone would come back? So I decided to go downstairs and get a glass of wine to help me sleep. Only, instead of going to the kitchen I walked to the window that looks down on my back-yard."

She shivered.

"Someone was standing there looking up at my bed-room."

He hated that he'd been right.

"You didn't call the police?"

"I started to. I had the phone in my hand, then I realized how much attention that would focus on me."

And why would that worry her?

"I went back upstairs, grabbed a couple of things, slipped out the front door and came here."

She shivered again despite a long dark coat that exposed a pair of slim white calves. Bare feet had been stuffed into a pair of slip-on deck shoes. He couldn't help wondering exactly what she was wearing under that coat. Her hair was a loose, velvety mass that fell around her face and shoulders. In one hand she had a death grip on a plastic shopping bag. The item sticking out of the top appeared to be her broken purse.

He flipped on the kettle.

"I don't want any tea. Thank you," she added as an afterthought.

Gabe shrugged. "No wine."

"That's okay, I'm not thirsty."

He didn't want her here. Even though he'd made the initial offer, he hadn't expected her to accept and now he was stuck. He could always turn her loose. But he knew he wouldn't.

"I'll show you the spare room."

She didn't move when he turned toward the stairs.

"Are you going to bed?"

Despite the darkness he saw her trepidation. It wasn't an act. She was afraid.

"No."

"I'm not sleepy, either."

Inwardly, he cursed. "I have to work, Cassiopia."

"That's okay. I've never watched an artist work. I won't get in your way."

It wasn't okay. She *would* be in the way. She'd be a distraction and he couldn't afford to be distracted any more tonight.

He thought of several responses but dismissed them. She was scared. So was he.

Someone had three vials of a toxin so deadly it could wipe out a city full of people in a matter of hours. The knowledge had eaten at him for nearly four years. Knowing that the authorities were concentrating on the wrong suspects had made it that much worse. Few people knew that *all* the toxin and all the documentation relating to it were missing.

The removable hard drives and Dr. Pheng's research notes had vanished from inside a locked vault on the base. Only a handful of people had access to that secured area and he and Beacher had been two of those people.

They had discussed this over beers in his workroom many nights. The way they had it figured, Gabe had been the designated patsy from the start. Most likely, he'd been intended to die in the explosion along with Dr. Richards. If Major Frank Carstairs hadn't died of a heart attack that same night, maybe they could have proved their suspicions, but as things stood, they had no living suspects, no proof and no trail to follow.

"Did you call Beacher?" Gabe asked her.

Cassiopia hesitated before nodding. "He isn't answering his phones."

So she had called Beacher first—if she wasn't lying. Gabe didn't think she was lying. Her fear was real. He scowled. Reluctantly, he motioned her to follow him.

CASSY GAVE AN EXASPERATED sigh as she tailed Gabriel's broad back down the stairs. She shouldn't have come. It was obvious he didn't want her here. She had plenty of friends she could have called. Why hadn't she?

Because he'd offered. And none of her friends would know what to do if someone came after her again. She couldn't place any of them at risk.

But she could have called the police.

She turned the thought aside as she carefully picked her way down the narrow staircase in his wake. "Forget to pay your electric bill?"

He reached the bottom without making a sound.

"Sometime you're going to have to tell me how you do that."

"Do what?"

"Step on that third step without making any noise."

She suspected he smiled, although she couldn't see his expression as he led her off to the left. She'd turned right before.

His workroom was cluttered and brightly lit. Her gaze instantly fastened on the clay taking shape on the largest table and she inhaled audibly. Even incomplete, the piece was magnificent.

"You have so much talent."

Looking embarrassed, he indicated the ratty old couch and un-upholstered wood chair in the far corner of the room next to an ancient, badly scarred desk and a battered filing cabinet. Exactly what she had been looking for. But if the toxin was hidden in this room, he wouldn't have led her here now.

"I have to finish this tonight."

"Okay." She ignored his impatience and stared around curiously at the crowded workspace. "Go ahead and work. You won't even know I'm here."

RIGHT. CASSIOPIA RICHARDS was the biggest distraction Gabe could imagine. How was he supposed to work with someone in the room? Whenever Beacher came over, Gabe always stopped, got a beer from the basement refrigerator and sat down to talk with him. He didn't have that sort of time tonight.

"There's beer," he told her gruffly with a nod toward the refrigerator.

"Thanks, but what I'd really like is a bathroom."

"Through there." He indicated the door at her back. She turned, still clutching her bag, and disappeared inside. For a moment he wondered if he should have searched the bag. He dismissed that thought as true paranoia and replaced the gun under the table. He must be insane.

He was working when she finally emerged with the coat slung over one arm. Whatever she'd been wearing beneath it had been replaced by the jeans she'd had on earlier tonight and a sweatshirt. Her hair was now clipped behind her ears, flowing down her back to emphasize the graceful curve of her neck.

Right. He was going to have no trouble concentrating now.

Without a word, she crossed to the refrigerator, hesitated over the selection and came out with a bottle of imported beer. Carrying everything to the worn green sofa, she sat on a sagging cushion.

A ton of questions crowded his mind, but the clock discouraged him from starting the sort of conversation they needed to have. He'd be lucky to complete the piece tonight as it was.

True to her word, Cassiopia remained silent. At first it was disconcerting to have her watch, but amazingly, his fingers continued to work, quick and sure, while his thoughts tumbled chaotically. After a while he was lost in the rhythm of his work.

His muscles had started a serious burn of protest by the time the final rose took shape beneath the tool in his tired fingers. It unnerved him to realize Cassiopia had been right. As impossible as it seemed, he *had* been able to ignore her presence.

Looking up, he found her with her head pillowed on her coat, fast asleep. Strands of silky hair covered most of her face. The partially emptied bottle of beer was on the corner of the desk, in danger of falling at the slightest jar.

Gabe rolled his shoulders to stretch tensed muscles and washed his hands before crossing the room to rescue the beer. It was warm and flat. He was too tired to be drinking alcohol, but he finished it, watching her sleep, and tried to ignore the faint stirring of desire.

She wouldn't appreciate his interest. Cassiopia had made her opinion of him clear. She had a lot in common with a rose. Soft and lovely to look at with plenty of thorns.

He couldn't see her with Beacher. Beacher liked his women delicate, plentiful and quick to fade. The thorny ones tended to get tossed back fast. Even ones as appealing as her.

Gabe pinched the bridge of his nose and carried the empty bottle to the recycle bin. Eyeing the finished piece critically he decided it was good. It might even be one of the best things he'd done.

For a moment he debated removing the tiny bee he'd added at the last minute. Somehow, it seemed a little too symbolic sitting on a petal, staring at an unopened bud as if wishing for what it couldn't have. But knowing he couldn't remove it without disturbing the work, Gabe began cleaning up. Cassiopia never stirred, even when he ran the shower in the bathroom next door.

Dumping his dirty clothes in the washer, he wrapped a towel around his waist and called to her gently. No response. There was no way he could carry her up two flights of stairs tonight. He wasn't sure he could carry himself to bed, as tired as he felt. It was going on five

and he had to be at Denny's with the bears that were cur-
rently cooling in his open kiln by eight.

In the laundry room he found a clean sheet and used
it to cover her. A good host would go up and bring her
down a blanket. He could live with being a lousy host.

He left a light on for her and headed upstairs. If she
decided to search his basement when she woke, she
wouldn't be the first. Like the others, she'd be doomed
to disappointment.

Chapter Four

Cassiopia was still asleep when Gabe went downstairs to take the cooled pair of bears from the kiln. He scrawled her a note on the back of one of his sketches and left it in plain sight on top of the desk. He hoped she'd have enough sense not to return to her town house.

There hadn't been a word from Beacher and he worried all the way to Denny's place in Hagerstown. The moldmaker was pleased with the bears, but he eyed Gabe with disfavor.

"You look like hell. You sick?"

"No." Exhausted, but there was no point telling the man that the little sleep he'd gotten in the past two days barely qualified as a nap.

"How's that custom piece for Rochelle coming along?"

"I finished sculpting it last night."

"Geez, boy. No wonder you look like that. You don't have to push yourself this hard."

Gabe shrugged. "I have a deadline."

"Didn't anyone tell you artists are supposed to be eccentric? She'll expect you to be late. She knows how hard you've been working to finish the show pieces."

Gabe didn't bother to respond. He'd agreed to Rochelle's deadline, so he'd make the deadline.

"You are one hardheaded cuss, you know that? When are you picking up the ark sets from the Bailin Brothers?"

"Next stop."

Denny nodded and eyed the pair of bears. "I still think you oughta consider doing some of these in cold cast. Resins sell well to the mass market."

"They'd have to be painted."

"Not necessarily, however, I know someone who could help you there. She'd work cheap."

Gabe's lips twisted ruefully. While the old man generally gave good advice and had taught him a great deal about his new career, Denny was a little too concerned with Gabe's lack of social life for comfort. He kept urging Gabe to get out and make new friends. Gabe would take bets the female artist who would "work cheap" was single and attractive, like Rochelle.

"I'll think about it," he temporized.

"You do that, boy. Your work's too fine to be collecting dust in some basement."

The words were uncomfortably close to what Cassiopia had told him only yesterday.

He had plenty of time to worry about her and Beacher on the drive into Pennsylvania to pick up the bronzed ark pieces from Tony Bailin. Tony and his brother, Max, did first-class work when it came to casting and they'd done so once again. Gabe liked the two men and enjoyed their company, but today, he found it hard to concentrate on their friendly conversation.

He decided to stop for a late lunch on the way home and used the time to try and reach Beacher again. Still no answer. Worry had become outright concern. It wasn't like Beacher not to return phone calls. Swinging by his friend's parking lot confirmed that Beacher's car still wasn't there.

Exhaustion vied with worry that was compounded the minute Gabe walked inside his house. Cassiopia was gone. She'd written *Thanks* in rounded letters beneath his note and signed it with a *C*. The sheet he'd covered her with was folded neatly beneath the paper sitting on the desk.

He'd have been surprised to find her still here yet it worried him all the same. He checked his caller ID for the number of her cell phone. When the call switched to voice mail he hung up. She'd probably gone to work. As tired as he was, he needed to do the same. Rochelle's people were due in less than an hour to start loading the show-pieces and he hadn't yet tagged the ones that were staying.

Gabe considered opening the package first, but if it did contain the missing toxin, he couldn't take the risk. As soon as the packers left he'd try Beacher one more time and then he'd see what his friend had in there.

Rochelle's men were friendly and efficient. They'd nearly finished crating and clearing the display room when Rochelle herself arrived and greeted him with her usual exuberant hug.

"I am not letting you have both crouching lions," he warned without preamble.

Rochelle contrived to look hurt. "I didn't come here for that, but I do wish you'd reconsider. Those lions are brilliant. They exemplify you *and* your work."

"No."

"As a pair, they'd be the highlight of the show."

"No."

The flicker of annoyance was accompanied by a toss of her head. "You're just like them."

"Cold and hard?"

"Fierce and determined. Never mind. Denny tells me you finished the chipmunks."

She was giving up far too easily. Nevertheless, he made the switch with her. "The piece will go in the kiln tonight."

"Great! May I see it? Ray and Dave can finish loading while we take a quick look."

He could hardly refuse since she'd commissioned it, however, he pointed out, "You aren't dressed for the workroom."

Despite the fact that it was late afternoon, the white linen suit Rochelle wore still looked crisp and fresh and expensive. While he kept a neat workspace, if she brushed against the wrong thing she'd spot the material. On the other hand, he'd never seen Rochelle anything but perfectly turned-out no matter what she was doing. Maybe dirt was afraid of her.

"Don't worry, I'll be careful."

He knew firsthand that her cheerful, outgoing manner hid a core of solid steel. With an *up to you* shrug, Gabe led her downstairs.

He was surprised by a tension that had nothing to do with getting her suit dirty. He hung back as she strode to the table and stared at the rosebush in silence for so long his jaw ached from clenching.

"I can't give this as a wedding gift."

His stomach plummeted.

"I want it. It's exquisite."

Relief swelled in his chest as his nerves stood down.

"We need to raise your prices."

"Feel free."

She tossed him a gleeful grin. "This is your best work yet, Gabe. I love the bumblebee! Great touch. As much as I adore my aunt and her chipmunk collection, I really think I have to keep this one for myself. I'm thinking a limited edition. Maybe seven. I, of course, want the first cast."

Her features grew serious as she tore her gaze from the piece. "Now then, we really need to talk about your coming to the opening tomorrow night."

"No."

She was one of the few people who could look him in the face without flinching or staring. As she did so now, her mouth pinched in frustration.

"Gabe, the artist needs to be there. My clients like to meet—"

"No."

Her lips thinned. "Have dinner with me."

Amused, he shook his head. "Feeding me won't change my mind."

"I got that. But there's one person you simply must meet."

She held up a hand when he would have refused.

"Before you say no, hear me out. Gretchen Morrison is important to both of us. She's one of my best clients. If she takes an interest in your work you won't be able to produce fast enough."

"My *work*," he emphasized, "not *me*."

"Gretchen is seventy-two. She's seen it all and she

isn't going to be put off by a scowl and a few scars. Trust me. She's wealthier than Midas and knows everyone there is to know on three continents. If you won't come to your opening you have to meet her tonight. She takes a personal interest in the artists she buys."

An excellent reason *not* to meet her. He already had far too many people interested in his personal life.

"I like my privacy."

"I know, but it's that important. Please, Gabe. She's stopping by the gallery at seven tonight. We'll grab an early dinner, talk about your next project and then you can stop by the showroom so I can go over how I plan to showcase the displays. You don't have to stay. Just say hello, nice to meet you, and then slip away. Please, Gabe," she repeated.

Mentally, he swore. He was dead tired but he owed Rochelle nearly as much as he owed Denny.

"I'm not doing the opening," he warned.

"I'll keep working on that, but this is more essential."

She would, too. She was like a bulldog when she wanted something. The stocky deliveryman called Dave stuck his head in the door before Gabe could refuse once more.

"We've loaded everything and we're heading out, Rochelle."

"Great. Tell Jennifer I'll be back in an hour or so."

The head vanished with a nod.

"You haven't met my new assistant, Jennifer Mackley, yet have you?" Rochelle asked as she started around the worktable.

"No." But he'd talked to the woman and was willing to take bets she was the sort who stared.

Rochelle paused to study the sketches and photographs pinned to the corkboard on the wall.

"Are these for your next project?"

He nodded. The series of wolves stared back at them.

"I want them."

He arched his eyebrow.

"Very commercial," she assured him. "They'll sell in a heartbeat." She stared at his notes. "Scale them down to no more than sixteen inches. I'm having more success with the smaller stuff right now. How soon can you get them finished? Have you thought about doing them in something other than bronze? Let's talk about it over dinner. I'm starving."

He let her sweep him outside to her silver Porsche at the curb. No car had ever looked more out of place in his quiet neighborhood. The truck and its crew were already gone. Rochelle gave him one of her exuberant hugs. His hands automatically steadied her as she leaned into him, smelling faintly of some wildly expensive perfume. He didn't feel even a stirring of desire for her.

"I'm so glad Denny found you for me. You're going to make us both very wealthy. See you at the restaurant. Is the Italian place near the gallery, okay?"

He hadn't agreed to dinner, but it was typical of Rochelle to take his assent for granted. He frowned, not wanting to go, but knowing an argument would take more time than simply going along. At his nod she climbed in and started the engine.

He'd always known Rochelle was beautiful, but until that moment, seeing her features in profile, he hadn't realized how much she reminded him of his former fiancée, Andrea Fielding. The thought was deeply unsettling. He waited until her taillights rounded the corner before he started for his bike.

THERE HADN'T BEEN TIME to run home and change before going to work when Cassy woke up in Gabe's basement, stiff from sleeping on his lumpy couch. Since she didn't have any meetings, she hoped her casual clothing wouldn't matter. Because she arrived at work so late, she clocked out late to make up the time. Not that she should have bothered showing up in the first place. She'd been too distracted all day to get any real work done.

It was almost dark when she pulled into her parking lot and eyed her town house with more than a little trepidation. Making certain no one loitered in the parking lot, she approached her front door nervously. Would she ever feel safe here again?

Of course she would. This was her home. She wasn't going to let some pervert scare her off.

As Cassy stepped inside the foyer something crunched under her shoe. Shutting the door, she flicked on the light and stared in horror at the wreckage of her home. Glass from the hall mirror near the door littered the floor. Mirrors, pictures, vases and ornaments all lay shattered amid the stuffing that had once been her treasured couch and chairs.

Shock left her stunned in disbelief. If it could break, it had been broken. If it could be sliced open, its fillings littered the carpeting. In the kitchen, the refrigerator and cupboards had been opened and their contents tossed. The mingled odors of spoiling food made her gag.

The person last night had done all this?

Horror gave way to fury. Marching up the stairs in rage and shock, she was inside her bedroom before the scene registered. The contents of her closet and one of her dresser drawers were scattered everywhere, but the devastation was incomplete, as if the person hadn't finished. The fully made bed looked ludicrous amid the mess. She crossed to it quickly, her hand sliding beneath the pillow, seeking the hard metal weapon she kept there.

Perhaps he made a slight noise, or maybe it subconsciously registered that her bathroom light was the only thing on in the house. Either way, Cassy sensed another presence before her eyes even lifted to the doorway across the bed from her. The figure was nothing more than a silhouette as she yanked her gun from under the pillow.

Cassy didn't realize she'd pulled the trigger until the sound reverberated in her ears.

The bullet slammed into the wall and the figure sprinted for the hall. Cassy glimpsed the blade of a long knife in one hand and fired again. The person continued to run. She started to give chase and stumbled over a pair of shoes on the floor. By the time she was on her feet again, the intruder was gone and the French door leading onto the back deck was standing open.

Fear hit her in a rush of blind panic. Cassy turned to the front door and ran for her car, shoving the gun in her coat pocket. She was halfway to Gabriel's house before she even realized that was where she was going.

Insane. She didn't even like the man, yet he represented safety.

A car horn honked loudly. Jerking the wheel, she

pulled back into her own lane, shaking all over. She was cold. So cold her teeth were chattering.

Reaction. Shock. She shouldn't be driving in this condition.

Cassy pulled the car to the side of the road and gave in to the trembling, but not the tears. She blinked back the angry moisture that filled her eyes. Who had done that to her home? Why?

She should have gone next door. Her neighbor was a cop. Neil would know what to do. Except, if he'd been home he would have heard the shots. He would have come to investigate.

And if she went to the police her employers were bound to find out. Bartlett Inc. had hired her when no one else would. As Powell Richards's daughter, she'd been tainted. No one wanted the authorities stopping by their place of business to ask her questions every few months. And no one wanted to worry about her loyalties. Only Justin Bartlett had been willing to take a chance. Cassy had done everything she could to keep a low profile and prove herself. She would not lose this job!

If she went to the police now her name alone would trigger a new investigation. A mugging was one thing, someone trashing her house afterward was going to set off all sorts of alarms. She couldn't afford to call the police even if it meant her insurance company wouldn't cover the damages.

Gabriel had been right. Someone thought she had the missing toxin. But why now, after all these years?

THERE WERE NO comforting shadows in Rochelle's brightly lit gallery. Jennifer Mackley's wide-eyed gaze of sympathetic horror was about what Gabe had expected. He wasn't surprised when she found a reason to be elsewhere as quickly as possible.

Gretchen Morrison, however, proved to be an outspoken woman with a piercing stare and a military carriage only slightly bowed with age. If Gabe had been into sculpting faces, hers would have been a must. Lined with grace and beauty, her indomitable character was clearly stamped in each feature. She stared hard at his scar and pursed lips thinned by time. She shook a head of soft, silvery hair.

"That must have hurt."

He tried not to show his surprise. Her bird-sharp gaze dropped to his hands.

"How'd you burn them?"

Amazingly, the abrupt question didn't bother him. Though his name was old news as far as the media was concerned, he had a feeling she knew exactly who he was and was testing his reaction. Years of military discipline kept him from giving her any outward reaction.

"Protecting my face."

She sniffed. "Not enough."

He nearly smiled. "No."

"Rochelle tells me you're good."

Unable to think of a suitable response, he twitched his shoulder in a tiny shrug. Approval came and went in those intelligent eyes. Gabe found himself liking the petite woman.

"Self-taught?"

He thought of his grandfather, who'd initially taught him the craft as a boy, and all the books and pictures he'd studied since therapy had opened this new path for him, but he inclined his head.

"The best usually are. We'll see."

The words were a clear dismissal. Gabe nearly went to parade rest. She turned away and began speaking with Rochelle. He gave it a minute, got on his motorcycle and slipped away while they were talking.

Beacher still wasn't answering his home, work or cell phones. Gabe wished he had a key to get into his friend's apartment. Every instinct he had was screaming that something was badly wrong. He might be able to talk his way in past the manager, but then what?

Frustrated and edgy, he changed direction, half tempted to drive over to Cassiopia's town house. That would serve no purpose, either. He'd done what he could for her.

So why was that thought so unsatisfying?

He should go home and open that package. Instead, he turned the bike toward the gym. The meal he'd had with Rochelle earlier was sitting heavily on his stomach. The package wasn't going anywhere and he wanted to give Beacher plenty of time to show up. Besides, he needed a physical release for all his pent-up frustration.

Gabe moved from machine to machine relentlessly, pushing himself until his muscles trembled with the strain and perspiration soaked his T-shirt and shorts. Even his few nodding acquaintances gave him a wide berth. A glance in the mirror after his shower explained why. His features were grim enough to make anyone think twice about approaching. His scar stood out prominently on his cheek, making him appear more dangerous and frightening than ever. No one said a word as he left the locker room.

As always, he was glad to leave the bright lights of

the gym for the welcoming shadows of the night. Though physically exhausted, he felt mentally charged. He'd work tonight. Instead of the wolf set, maybe a baying coyote. It was more suited to his mood.

He was sketching the animal in his mind as he rounded the corner of his street and saw the government car sitting out front. Fear clawed its way up his throat. He should have gone straight home. If they'd made one of their unofficial raids and found the package and it contained what he was beginning to fear it might, he was going down hard and final.

He would not believe that Beacher had set him up. If he couldn't trust Beacher there was no one left in the world he *could* trust.

Gabe swore softly. He'd refused to let Rochelle have both crouching lions for the show. Now he regretted that decision. While extremely well-disguised, the hidden compartment in the ornately carved base of the one would reveal its presence under a close examination. It would have been far better if Rochelle had been the one to find the package.

Gabe was tempted to keep driving, but that would only delay the inevitable. The military was boldly announcing their presence. Did that mean they had a warrant this time?

He drove past the two men inside the parked car and pulled around back. Going in through the kitchen, he didn't have time to remove his jacket before they were ringing the front doorbell.

He'd expected Len Sliffman, but he was startled to see his former superior officer standing there. Time hadn't been kind to Captain Bruce Huntington—now Major Bruce Huntington. The man was thin to the point of emaciation, with less hair on his close-cropped dome than Gabe remembered. The commanding lines that had once framed his mouth and eyes were now unforgiving wrinkles that gave his face a permanently sour expression. Bitter dislike still burned in the pale blue eyes that met Gabe's. Huntington viewed rules with almost religious fervor. Gabe was a frequent sinner in his eyes.

Beside him, Len Sliffman looked years younger than he actually was. Bulky with muscle rather than fat, his thatch of brown hair was neatly combed in a standard FBI cut, even though the former agent had worked with Homeland Security since its inception. He'd been part of the original team of investigators four years ago and, while expected, his presence beside the major caused Gabe's stomach to clench.

The package loomed in his thoughts as he greeted them.

"Got a warrant?"

Huntington's ramrod back stiffened. Sliffman merely shook his head. "We were hoping for conversation without doing this the hard way."

While tempted to keep them standing there, Gabe widened the opening and stepped back. The men crowded into his small hall. He didn't invite them to sit or come in any farther.

"What do you know about Cassiopia Richards?" Huntington demanded.

Gabe's relief was profound. They weren't here because of the package. He tried not to show the fact by so much as a muscle twitch. If they were asking about

Cassiopia, he must have missed a watcher outside the other night.

"She's Powell Richards's daughter."

"Don't get smart."

"You ought to try it some time." With a feral smile that was all teeth and no humor, Gabe slouched back against the wall, both to put himself in deeper shadow and because he knew his posture would infuriate Huntington.

It did. The major's scowl deepened. Hands fisted at his sides. The fact that he ignored the jibe set off a whole new set of alarms in Gabe.

"How *well* do you know her?"

Wrong question. What was going on?

"She believes I murdered her father. How well do you think I know her?"

Huntington spit the next question past a clenched jaw.

"When did you see Beacher Coyle last?"

"Nice of you to be so interested in my social life, Major, but I don't see that it's any of your business."

Fear crawled in his belly.

Huntington closed the distance between them. Gabe allowed the other man to get right up in his face. Déjà vu, except that Gabe was no longer under his command and wasn't the least bit intimidated. He forced himself to remain slouched against the wall while his brain raced to puzzle out the reason behind this line of questions.

"It became my business when he was found dead tonight, mister."

The words crashed over him. Gabe jerked upright,

nearly knocking against the major, who took a hasty step back. Horror and disbelief left Gabe mentally reeling.

"You're lying." He had to be lying.

"You didn't know."

Sliffman's quiet statement barely penetrated the dark haze filling his mind. Gabe stared unseeing at the pair while pain roared through him.

Not Beacher. God, not Beacher.

"It made the news." Huntington turned to growl impatiently at Sliffman. "How could he not have known?"

Gabe glided forward causing Huntington to take several more quick steps back.

"How?"

Sliffman stepped between them. "I'm sorry." The man's features softened. "He was murdered."

"Where have you been, Lowe?" Huntington demanded.

"Let me handle this, Bruce."

"Well, where's he been? Everyone knows he rarely leaves his house. And the two of them—"

"Shut up."

Another time Gabe might have appreciated the way Sliffman dealt with the major, but he could barely think past the talons of grief sunk deep in his soul.

No more beers and conversation to while away the hours. No more handball games at the gym. Beacher was dead. And the cause was most likely inside the package in his basement.

Beacher was dead.

He couldn't wrap his mind around it. How could Beacher be dead? The wrench of pain was intolerable.

Why hadn't he let Gabe watch his back if he was doing something dangerous?

Why hadn't he told Gabe what he was doing?

"He was on the floor in his bedroom. His throat was slit."

Gabe swayed. Sliffman reached out to steady him. Gabe battled to contain the contents of his stomach. He swallowed hard and jerked free.

Sliffman waited until he was steady before stepping back. "Powell Richards's daughter was seen running from his apartment before the police arrived."

Gabe jerked his head like a boxer who'd taken one blow too many. He tried to focus on the words.

Huntington snarled. "They aren't releasing that information, Len."

"Lowe didn't kill Coyle and we need his help."

"The hell we do! We need answers and this bastard is going to give them to us."

Beacher was dead.

"Shut up or leave, Bruce. You're only here in an advisory capacity because the military wanted someone sitting in who knew the principals. I'm in charge."

Gabe shunted his pain aside and focused on Sliffman. "What does Cassiopia Richards have to do with his murder?"

Sliffman shook his head. "We don't know. We'll ask her when we find her."

"You think she killed him?"

"Unlikely."

"Unless you helped her," Huntington added viciously.

Sliffman whirled, an oath on his lips. Gabe stopped him.

"*When* was he killed?"

"The medical examiner will have to determine the exact time of death, but it looks like sometime yesterday."

Beacher had been dead for twenty-four hours and Gabe hadn't known.

"Got an alibi, Lowe?" Huntington mocked.

Gabe forced his brain to concentrate, not feel. "No."

Creases of pleasure bracketed Huntington's features. Gabe addressed Sliffman.

"I worked all day yesterday. I didn't even go to the gym. I took a walk through the neighborhood last night instead."

"Anyone see you?"

Cassiopia. And it wouldn't take them long to learn about his confrontation with the local police at her place. However, if he told them about it now he'd be in for a long night of questioning. He needed to get downstairs and open that package first.

"It's possible I was noticed, but it was dark and I didn't stop to talk with anyone. I came home and worked until nearly five this morning. Around seven I drove to Hagerstown to drop off a piece to be molded. Afterward, I drove to Greensboro, Pennsylvania, to pick up some finished bronzes for the exhibit."

"Exhibit, huh?" Huntington sneered. "Moving up in the world?"

Gabe continued to ignore him and focused on Sliffman. "I can give you names, numbers and addresses. They can supply the times. Who found him?"

"An anonymous caller reported a disturbance," Sliffman told him.

"We're the ones asking the questions, Lowe," Huntington blustered.

Sliffman ignored him. "Coyle's apartment was tossed. Any idea what someone was looking for?"

"No." Gabe pictured his friend's pristine apartment and set his jaw. The killer had been looking for the package. Who else besides Cassiopia knew Beacher gave it to him? Had she murdered Beacher before coming to Gabe?

His mind raced. Technically he didn't *know* what was in the package, but he was walking a razor-thin line until he found out.

"When did you see Mr. Coyle last?" Sliffman asked, still calmly.

"Two nights ago. He stopped by for a beer."

"Was he upset?"

He'd been tense and agitated. Gabe had known something was wrong. He should have pushed Beacher for answers.

"What did he talk about?" Huntington inserted before Gabe could decide how to respond.

"I don't remember. He didn't stay long. He often stopped by." Which they would know from past observation. Beacher had made no secret of his friendship with Gabe despite its effect on his career. He'd lost his security clearance and been forced to resign from his job in the face of their suspicions. He'd been lucky to find another security firm that would hire him.

"He didn't seem upset?" Sliffman pursued again.

"He barely stayed long enough to finish his beer. I think he was meeting someone."

"Who?"

"He didn't say. A woman most likely." And that, too, they would know.

"His fiancée," Huntington supplied with a smirk.

Gabe couldn't mask his surprise. Cassiopia hadn't lied? He risked the proffered thread.

"He never mentioned a fiancée."

Huntington's grin was malicious. "I'm not surprised."

"Bruce," Sliffman cautioned.

"It's been on the news, Len. He might as well hear it from us. Your buddy got himself engaged to your former fiancée, Andrea Fielding."

Chapter Five

Huntington was too pleased with himself to be lying. He believed what he was saying. They would hammer at Gabe for hours if he let them. Gabe had no intention of letting them. The police would come next. Murder, after all, was their jurisdiction.

"Out."

Huntington brightened. "We can take you in right now."

Gabe nodded. "I'm done talking." Jaw clamped, he held Sliffman's gaze, letting the man see he meant every word.

"We need your help, Lieutenant Lowe."

And Gabe knew Sliffman had used his former title deliberately, reminding him of past loyalties.

"I know you don't want to consider this, but Beacher Coyle may have framed you four years ago."

Mutely, Gabe shook his head. His gaze never left Sliffman's, even when Huntington began goading him once more.

"Sure. He had the skills to rig that explosion just like you did. And he had access to the lab. Coyle could have taken the missing hard drives and research notes. He's probably been sitting on everything all this time, laughing while pretending to be your friend. He sells them to the highest bidder and walks away with your woman, your career and your reputation."

"Bruce…" Sliffman warned without looking away.

"But he screwed up, Lowe. The buyer didn't want to pay. You should see the body. Messed him up real bad."

It took every ounce of control Gabe had not to plant his fist in Huntington's face. Both men braced as he began to move. Sliffman's hand started toward his belt and the gun he no doubt had tucked there.

Gabe reached for the knob and threw the front door open before Sliffman could complete the action. Their gazes locked once more as Huntington began to bluster.

"You can't throw us out, Lowe. Under the Patriot Act we can haul your ass in right now and bury you so deep—"

"Shut up, Bruce. Let's go."

"Go? We need to search his house."

Gabe stood mute, letting his expression speak for him.

Homeland Security had lots of room to maneuver, but this situation was tricky and they all knew it. Murder was a police investigation first. Gabe had made it as clear as possible that he wouldn't cooperate with them.

He took what bitter pleasure he could from Huntington's astounded expression as Sliffman gave him a shove toward the open door.

"You can't be serious! We need to—"

Sliffman pulled a business card from an inside breast pocket. "When you've had some time, call me."

Gabe made no move to accept the extended card.

Sliffman let it fall to the floor. With a hard shove at the still spluttering Huntington, they were outside. Gabe locked the door behind them and ran for the basement. They'd be back with the police and a warrant. He had little time.

If Beacher was dead it was because he'd finally found the missing toxin, or someone thought he had. Recriminations were nothing new to Gabe, but thoughts of what he should have done and said to Beacher would haunt him forever. Beacher's death left a hollow void so overwhelming Gabe felt ill.

Ruthlessly, he pushed that aside. He couldn't change anything. But he could find the person responsible.

He raced down the stairs without light, only flicking the switch when he hit the display room door. He jerked to an abrupt stop. Heart thudding, he stared at the empty spot on the floor where one of the crouching lions should have still been waiting for him.

Blind panic assailed him before rational thought kicked in.

Rochelle!

He'd known she'd given up too easily. She'd come in person this afternoon to distract him so her men could carry both lions out to the van. She would claim her men had made a mistake but since she already had them…

Gabe reached for his cell phone then swore. By now her gallery was closed. Even if he got Rochelle to open it for him, he didn't want a witness or questions when he removed the package.

Sliffman was leaning toward believing Gabe had nothing to do with Beacher's murder, but the man was a professional. Gabe would be under constant surveillance from now on. The last thing he wanted was to draw official attention to the lions.

Swearing under his breath, Gabe used his cell phone to call Rochelle's number.

"You took both crouching lions," he told her answering machine coldly. "I want them returned, first thing in the morning. Both of them."

He was fairly certain she wouldn't return his call tonight. She'd do everything she could to keep them for tomorrow's opening.

Assuming the panel they'd built into the ebony base hadn't already been discovered, the package was safer inside Rochelle's gallery than it would be here tonight even if it meant learning the contents would have to wait.

The chain of evidence would be muddied if the lions and the package sat in a public forum for a few days. On the other hand, the person who murdered Beacher was unlikely to sit around and wait. Gabe needed to prepare for unwanted company.

Striding to the workroom he pulled down the gun and spare shells he had taped to the underside of the work-table. He owned two guns that were legally registered to him and had been for over nine years. Unless they were total incompetents, the authorities knew about them and where he kept them. He stuck this one in his belt. The shell casings went into his jacket pocket.

He was too restless and upset to work tonight, but he moved the completed rosebush to the kiln. He was heading for the stairs when there was a muffled thump overhead. Gun in hand, he silently took the stairs by twos.

A second thump and the clatter of a chair against the

dining room table was followed by a soft curse. Gabe returned the gun to his waistband and strode forward to greet his intruder.

"I'm going to have to get that window fixed."

CASSY GAVE A STARTLED YELP. Her penlight flash fastened on the immovable chest that suddenly filled the kitchen doorway. She stopped in the process of untangling her long coat from the chair.

"Gabriel! You scared me! Don't you ever use lights?"

"More often than apparently you use doors."

"That isn't funny."

"I agree."

Her heart continued to leap and thud erratically. "I didn't think you were home. I didn't want anyone to see me standing on your front porch."

"Like the police?"

The flatness in his voice raised goose bumps along her arms. This wasn't simply anger. He was furious, and from the suppressed grief she detected in his tone, he already knew about Beacher.

"You heard. I'm so sorry."

His expression didn't alter by so much as a flicker of emotion.

"You were there."

The words were cold and flat. Cassy shuddered as the horrific memory filled her mind.

"Yes." Bile rose in her throat. She'd had hours to deal with it, but she doubted she'd ever forget a single detail of that room and that smell. They were etched permanently in the wall of her mind.

"Did you kill him?"

"Of course not!"

"Why are you here?" His tone was hard, unyielding.

"Beacher trusted you. That makes you someone I can trust as well."

"One does not follow the other."

Belatedly, she recognized the cold menace in him. Like any wounded beast the lion was fully roused and poised to strike out. Cassy wasn't sure why his anger was directed at her, but she sensed that if she showed the slightest trace of fear he'd rip her to shreds.

"Save your angry lion impression for later." She hated the slight quiver in her voice. "I know you care."

"About you?"

"Hardly. But Beacher was your friend. You want to find out who murdered him as much as I do."

"You're the chief suspect."

"What?"

He ignored her startled yelp. He was serious!

"According to Homeland Security, you were seen leaving his apartment."

Who had seen her there? How had anyone known who she was? Were the authorities following her? That had been the case right after her father died, but she'd thought the shadowing had stopped a long time ago.

"You can't really believe I had anything to do with his murder."

"You'd be surprised by what I believe."

The beam bobbled in her hand. It was shaking. *She* was shaking. She couldn't afford to let his rage get to her.

"I had nothing to do with Beacher's murder. I went to him for help."

"Why?"

Exasperation filled her. "Because of what happened to my house! I've been calling him for days."

And Beacher had been dead at least some of that time. She was angry and scared and tired of being afraid.

"Believe what you want. I drove to his apartment and a couple leaving let me into the building. I was determined to make him talk to me. He didn't answer when I knocked so I tried the handle. The door was unlocked."

She drew a deep breath and tried for calm as the images surged forward. "His place looked like mine, it had been torn to shreds. He was there." She shuddered. "Dead."

"What do you mean—? Never mind. Why come here?"

"I don't know where else to go."

Did he have any idea what it had cost her to admit that? He studied her from the shadows. She was still prey.

"Bad choice," he told her finally. "My house is under surveillance."

Fear fluttered in her chest. He reached for her arm and she realized she'd swayed. She felt the warmth of those firm fingers even through her coat and sweatshirt.

"Come on."

"Where?"

"Away from here."

Well that was clear as mud, but his steely grip left her little choice. He hauled her into the kitchen and released her to open a cupboard. Taking down an opened box of cereal, he dumped half a box's worth of contents into the sink and turned on the disposal. Then he plunged his hand inside the empty box. He withdrew a white envelope that appeared stuffed with cash and shoved it into a pocket.

"Wait here."

Cassy shivered as the past forty-eight hours began crashing down on her. She should leave, but before she could make her legs carry her to the back door he returned.

"Put this on." He held out a man's jacket. "Hurry."

Arguing seemed inadvisable in the face of that grim countenance. She took off her coat and remembered her gun. As he glanced out the back door, she moved it from the pocket of her coat to the jacket pocket, marveling that she was responding without questioning him. Why did he want her to wear the jacket? What was he doing? What was *she* doing? She should leave, but she dropped her coat on the table.

"Let's go."

"Where?" she repeated, tugging on the jacket. His only response was to tell her not to make another sound.

His urgency was contagious. While her mind questioned everything, renewed adrenaline filled her. She'd already been scared. His tension invited a sense of near panic.

"No noise," he warned.

He opened the back door without a sound and reached for her hand. Cassy welcomed his warm touch against her icy skin. Her teeth chattered as he closed and locked the door before leading her into the vast shadows covering his yard.

Cassy couldn't see a thing. A horde of people could have stood there and she wouldn't have known. Clouds obscured what light the night sky might have offered and they were too far from the street and other houses for those lights to reach back here. But apparently lions could see in the dark.

When he stopped moving she bumped into him. He steadied her and she realized his motorcycle was in front of them. He pressed a finger lightly to her lips to indicate continued silence. Then he placed her hand on the back of his jacket. What was he doing?

Gabriel began to roll the motorcycle across the grass of his yard. That made no sense. There was a waist-high fence behind his house. She knew. She'd climbed the thing tonight. She'd found no gate, yet he was heading straight for the fence.

One of them was crazy and she was pretty sure it was her. What was she doing here?

Where else could she go?

She stopped when he stopped. He turned toward her and lowered his head. For a split second she had the insane notion that he was about to kiss her. Her heart skipped a beat but he rested his lips against her ear.

"Hold this."

She quivered as he handed off the heavy weight of the motorcycle to her. It was all she could do to keep it from toppling when he moved away. The clean scent of him seemed to linger on the night air.

She was definitely going insane.

Cassy couldn't see what he was doing, almost noiselessly, there in the dark, but abruptly Gabriel returned, took the weight of the bike back from her cold fingers and wheeled it through a peeled back section of wood fencing. Cassy followed. Once again she waited with the bike while he replaced the fencing.

She wanted to tell him her car was parked another street over, but she couldn't bring herself to break the silence. They had reached the corner of the yard between two brightly lit houses when a tremendous explosion ripped apart the stillness of the night.

Cassy whirled. Flames licked hungrily at the upstairs window of Gabriel's house.

"Hurry!" he commanded, plopping a helmet on her head.

Her shocked body obeyed automatically. They ran with the bike to the street. She expected Gabe to jump on and start it the minute they reached the pavement, but they continued moving until they came to the street corner. A dim streetlight cast faint shadows from the trees overhead. Only then did he swing onto the bike.

"My car—"

"No."

There was no arguing with that tone and this didn't strike her as a good time to mention that she'd never ridden a motorcycle in her life. She let him haul her up roughly behind him and threw her arms around his waist. Her feet found their place as he started the engine with a deafening roar. There was nothing to do but close her eyes and hold on tight as they tore down the deserted street.

Her thoughts spun, as chaotic as the ride itself. Once they hit the main street he weaved between cars as if they were nothing more than an obstacle course.

Before she realized his intent, they were on the interstate heading south. All she could do was concentrate on staying on the bike. Death seemed the most likely outcome of this crazed ride, but since there was nothing she could do to prevent it, she closed her eyes and prayed the end would be relatively painless.

By the time he pulled onto city streets once more, her entire body felt as numb as her mind. It was anticlimactic when he finally stopped near the entrance to a motel parking lot. She thought they were somewhere in Virginia but she wasn't sure.

"The scars make me noticeable. You're going to have to rent the room. One room. Ask for the ground floor."

One room? That penetrated. If he thought she was sharing a bed with him he was in for a rude surprise. Even as she formed an appropriate protest, he shoved several bills in her hand.

"One night, in cash."

"They'll want a credit card."

"They won't care as long as you pay up front."

He swung her off the bike, scooped the helmet off her head and placed it on his own.

"Go."

Cassy went. What else could she do? She was terrified, confused and too exhausted to think straight. Had he blown up his own house as a diversion? The very thought terrified her.

The two clerks behind the counter were young, female and friendly. Cassy heard herself explaining she and her boyfriend had been robbed while on their way home to Pennsylvania. The women were so nice she felt guilty, but she took the emergency supplies they offered including combs, toothbrushes and toothpaste.

Outside, Cassy handed Gabriel one of the key cards. She couldn't see his features behind the helmet, but she thought he was eyeing the items in her hand.

"What was that all about?"

"I told them we were robbed. They gave me some supplies."

He made no comment and she allowed him to haul

her back up on the bike. He steered them around to the rear of the building where a more dimly lit entrance led inside. The room itself seemed cramped, dwarfed as it was by the huge bed. A scarred table sat between two coarsely stuffed armchairs in front of the bank of windows. Cassy collapsed gratefully into the nearest chair, relieved to be sitting on something that didn't move.

Gabriel immediately closed the drapes. He prowled the room like a stalking beast, checking the bathroom and the small wardrobe. Did he expect someone to jump out at them? Finally satisfied, he tossed his helmet on the bed and finished surveying the room critically.

"Aren't you going to check under the bed, too?"

He glared at her. Cassy didn't care. She was beyond intimidation now. "You want to tell me what happened back there?" she demanded.

His scowl raised the hairs on her arms.

"The house blew up."

That said, he disappeared into the bathroom, closing the door with an audible snap.

As a conversational stopper the move was effective. It also reminded Cassy that her bladder had been shaken thoroughly. She stared at her reflection in the mirror over the dresser. No wonder the clerks hadn't questioned her story. Shadows rimmed eyes that were sunken with fatigue and fear. Her skin had a pallid, blotchy look while her hair was a tangled, listless mop. The ill-fitting black suede jacket was twin to the one Gabriel was wearing. Both were perfectly suited to riding a motorcycle for miles.

Gabriel came out a few minutes later and she seized

the room for her own needs without comment. She was a mature adult. A chemical engineer with a Ph.D. She'd escaped an attacker twice, seen the mutilated remains of a man she'd known briefly and now she was running from the authorities. Sharing a room for the night with a man who didn't even like her would be a piece of cake.

As long as it was on her terms.

She checked the coat pocket to be sure she still had her wallet and the nine-millimeter semiautomatic she'd purchased after her father had died. Once it had given her a measure of security to learn how to use the weapon even though she'd never really expected to need the knowledge.

If Gabriel Lowe thought he had some helpless little woman on his hands, he was in for a surprise.

After running a wet cloth over her face and doing what she could with one of the combs, Cassy decided it was time to face the lion in *their* den.

The room was empty.

She allowed panic to have its moment until she spotted his helmet in the center of the bed. Surely he would have taken it with him if he weren't planning to return. Either he'd gone out to his bike for something or—

The door swung open. Cassy jumped. Her hand went to her coat pocket. Gabriel stepped inside juggling an ice bucket and several canned drinks from the vending machine they'd passed down the hall.

"Limited choices. They don't run to beer or wine."

She expelled a breath and released her grip on the gun while he set everything on the table. He took a glass, added ice and popped the tab on a can of apple juice.

"Have a seat."

"Enough is enough!" She gave him her darkest glare. "I suppose you mean that to be a step up from 'sit.'"

She'd surprised him. Good.

"Did you blow up your house as a diversion?"

She tried not to cringe at the sweep of fury that crossed his face. He gripped the glass in his hand. It was easy to imagine he was picturing her neck there instead.

"No." He took a long swallow of his drink.

"But you knew it was going to blow up."

"No."

"Then why did you rush us out of there right before it happened?"

He folded into the chair nearest the corner without responding. His silence was every bit as unnerving as he probably intended it to be.

"Okay. Enough! I mean it! I'm suitably in awe of you, all right? You can skip the one-syllable answers. They aren't going to raise my fear quotient any higher. I think I topped out when you pulled onto the interstate."

She was positive she saw a flicker of amusement before his eyes returned to their usual impenetrable stare.

"Please sit down and join me," he offered dryly.

"Much better."

Weak-kneed, she took the opposite chair and reached for the can of diet cola. She was proud of the fact that her fingers barely shook at all. She added ice to the second glass and poured the cola over top. He waited until she finished taking a swallow before speaking.

"Tell me what happened," he demanded.

"It was your house."

"To Beacher," he amended.

Cassy took another hasty swallow. The fizzy drink

nearly made her choke. Images of the blood-soaked body caused the trembling to start again. Pretending to be detached was beyond her. She would forever remember the stench of death.

"I didn't recognize him. His throat… There was so much blood. He was on the floor in his bedroom." She swallowed hard.

"Why did you leave my house this morning?"

Cassy scrambled to follow the question. "I was late for work. Your note didn't say when you were coming back."

"You worked all day?"

"I even stayed late to make up lost time. I'm in the middle of an important project right now and… It doesn't matter. I'm rambling."

"You went to Beacher's after you left work?"

"No! No," she amended less shrilly. She took a calming breath before continuing. "I went home. I know it was stupid," she agreed before he could point out the obvious, "but I needed to change clothes. I figured it was long odds that anyone would still be there."

He stilled. "You were wrong?"

She nodded bleakly. "The house was trashed, like Beacher's apartment and…"

"What was he looking for, Cassiopia?"

She clenched the glass more tightly. "It all comes back to that missing toxin, doesn't it?"

Gabriel scowled. "Why would anyone believe you had it after all these years?"

"I don't know."

"Not good enough."

Exhaustion tugged at her. Beacher had finally convinced her that Gabriel might be innocent. His death seemed to confirm that. Either she trusted this grim-faced man or she didn't.

"I think it must be because of Beacher."

"Your fiancé?"

She hated that he was baiting her.

"You know he was never my fiancé."

Gabriel inclined his head. For the first time, Cassy realized he'd turned off all the lights except the one on the table between them. While she'd been in the bathroom he'd positioned his chair so his features were mostly in shadow, as usual. That got on her remaining nerve.

"You really are into this whole creature of the night thing, aren't you?"

"What?"

She waved a hand to encompass the room. "Mood lighting. Shadows to give you a more sinister appearance, a surfeit of silence. What is it with you, anyhow? I've seen your scars, Gabriel. Impressive. Now get over it or go find a decent plastic surgeon. We've got bigger problems. I told you, I passed my scare quotient for the day."

She was pretty sure she saw respect in his eyes.

"Beacher found the vials, didn't he?" she continued. "He found them and gave them to you. Do you know what will happen when the fire department puts water on that fire back at your place?" She couldn't prevent another shudder. "Because I don't, but I can make a guess. They said that stuff multiplies and releases in liquid. If the toxin was in your house—"

"It wasn't."

Relief was a wave that nearly left her giddy. "Beacher didn't find the vials?"

"I don't know."

She slumped. "I was so sure. He looked so excited the last time I talked to him. He wasn't answering my calls so I assumed he took whatever he found to you."

For what felt like a long time Gabriel regarded her. She could almost hear his mind whirling.

"Not to the authorities?"

That gave her pause. "I don't know. I didn't even consider that possibility, but you're right, he would have gone to the military or Homeland Security, wouldn't he?"

"No."

There was no compromise in his tone.

"Why do you think he found anything, Cassiopia?"

"He's dead, isn't he?"

She could have bitten her tongue. She sensed the well of his grief even though it was impossible to read his stern features.

"I'm sorry. I didn't mean—"

"He gave me a wrapped package," Gabriel acknowledged before she could finish her apology, "but it wasn't in the house tonight."

"Where is it?"

"Safe."

"Stop with the cryptic! Did he find the toxin or not?"

"I don't know."

He spread his hands to forestall the blistering words forming on her lips.

"He gave me a package and asked me to hold it without questions. He said he'd explain when he came back."

"You didn't peek?"

"No."

Of course not. She was starting to understand that

Gabriel had a rigid code of honor. Beacher was his friend. Gabriel wouldn't have looked inside without permission.

"I went to check it after I learned he was dead and it was gone."

Panic clawed her throat. "Someone took it?"

"In a manner of speaking. I know where it is."

"Where?"

His expression didn't change. "Later."

"Don't you dare go all cryptic on me again!"

He hesitated a beat.

"Why should I trust you?"

Chapter Six

Satisfied he had her complete attention, Gabe nodded. "Someone is playing for keeps."

"I know that!"

"Do you really?"

"I *saw* what they did to Beacher."

He leaned back in his chair, thrusting aside his guilt and anger.

"Did you call the police?"

"Of course I did! I couldn't just leave him lying there. I called them from my car anonymously."

"From your cell phone."

"Yes, why?"

Gabe didn't bother to answer. The police hadn't needed an eyewitness to her presence at the murder scene. She'd told them she was there with her cell phone call. With a grimace, he changed the subject.

"You said someone trashed your house. Why didn't you call the police tonight? Or your neighbor, the cop."

She looked at him wearily. "Because after that man came out of the bathroom—"

He straightened, leaning forward. "He was still there?"

"Yes. This guy came out of the bathroom in full ninja attire. I nearly had a heart attack. He hadn't finished trashing my room or he'd have found the gun under my pillow. That's why I didn't end up like Beacher."

Gabe stared at her. "You shot him?"

"*At* him," she corrected. "I'm a lousy shot. He ran and so did I. If Neil had been home he'd have heard the shots and come running. He didn't and the truth is, I panicked. I just wanted to get away."

He believed her. Cassiopia was full of surprises. He never knew what she was going to do or say next.

"You're sure it was a man?"

"In that outfit it could have been an alien from Mars. The person was thin but I couldn't even tell you how tall he was."

As descriptions went, it sucked.

"Look, I'm sorry, okay? My goal was to get away. We need to see what Beacher gave you."

"It's out of reach until tomorrow."

"Why?"

He didn't answer, still not sure how much he wanted to tell her. "Why do you think he found the missing vials?"

"Don't you?" Cassy closed her eyes. "Beacher's been after me to talk to him for years now. I wouldn't because…"

"He was my friend."

She sighed. "Frankly, yes. Everyone believed the two of you were guilty and so did I. Do you have any idea how hard it is for me to believe my father was capable of taking something that deadly from his lab in the first place? The authorities implied someone might have been threatening to harm me to coerce him, but no matter what pressure or incentive was brought to bear on him, I would have said he was incapable of such a thing. Yet they are convinced he was the only one at Sunburst who could have removed those things from the vault."

Gabe knew security had been tight at the lab. He'd gone over the procedures himself. Her father must have been the one who removed the vials and the backup hard drive.

"Your father had no ties to any known terrorist group, no bones to pick with the government, so he would have needed a compelling reason to commit an act of treason."

His agreement rocked her back.

"But *would* he have taken the toxin to protect you?"

Her face pinched in pain. "My mother died of a heart attack two weeks before this happened. Dad was devastated. All we had left was each other. As much as I don't like admitting the possibility, I believe he would have done just about anything to keep me safe." She held up a palm. "Anything except steal something like this for a group of terrorists. I cannot—will not—believe he'd do something like that without telling someone in authority."

Gabe tensed. "Me."

"Yes. No!" She took a calming breath. "Dad didn't know you. If someone had threatened me he'd have gone to the head of security at Sunburst Labs."

"Arthur Longstreet?"

Cassy started to nod and stopped. "Arthur Longstreet was new then. I forgot. Frank Zimmer retired before Mom died. I don't think my dad knew the new man very well."

"And he didn't know me."

"No, but he knew Major Carstairs and Dr. Pheng."

"You think he went to Pheng?"

"Dr. Pheng said no when the authorities asked him."

"And Major Carstairs wasn't around to ask anymore."

Cassiopia stared at him.

"How well did your father know Carstairs?"

"They weren't close friends. I know they belonged to the same golf club and played together a few times."

"And Pheng?"

"Dad and Dr. Pheng went to school together."

Pheng wasn't particularly tall, but he was lean and athletic for his age.

"If someone did threaten me, Dad would have wanted protection. Dr. Pheng couldn't have arranged that, so I think he would have called the major."

"And Carstairs would have called me," Gabe agreed.

"Did he? Is that why you went there that day?"

Gabe fell silent. The major might well have ordered him to go to her father's home if there had been a threat, but there were other things he would have done as well and he hadn't.

Gabe leaned farther back into the shadows. He worked to keep emotion from his face and his voice.

"I don't remember anything about that day."

Cassiopia stared in shock. "Nothing?"

"No."

He'd hoped the hard, inflexible tone of his voice left no room for discussion. He should have known better.

"I find that hard to believe."

"So does everyone else," he agreed grimly.

"I've heard of severe trauma bringing on amnesia, but I never met anyone with such a condition."

"Guess I'm your first."

A hint of color deepened her cheeks.

"My dad wouldn't remove those vials and the research from the lab even to protect me."

"Unless he was ordered to do so."

The flat words lay between them.

"By Major Carstairs?"

"The major should have notified me immediately and sent reinforcements if there was a threat. He should have alerted the base commander and my direct supervisor. Homeland Security would have been alerted. None of that happened."

"Because he had a heart attack!"

"Not until after your dad's house exploded."

Cassiopia inhaled sharply. "Are you saying the major had something to do with the theft?"

Gabe picked his words carefully. "I think his death would have been a lot more suspect if Carstairs hadn't recently been diagnosed with heart trouble. He was up for promotion and instead he was going to wash out. You know there are drugs that can be used to encourage a fatal heart attack. Drugs that wouldn't necessarily show in an autopsy unless someone went looking for them."

Cassiopia looked stunned. "You're saying he was murdered? By who?"

"The same person who stole the vials, the hard drives and the research notes."

Cassiopia fell silent for several seconds. "Did you ever wonder about Beacher?"

"No," he lied. Because he *had* wondered at first. Trust

had been impossible for a long time after Gabe had regained enough sense to understand what had happened.

"I know you're friends—were friends—but hear me out. What if Beacher *was* involved? What if that's why he stayed so close to you all these years?"

"No."

"When we talked he suggested my father might have pretended to steal the vials and the research and switched them, hiding the real toxin."

Gabe nodded. "We discussed the possibility. If someone threatened you and he took the threat seriously and called Carstairs, it's possible Carstairs ordered your father to bring everything back to the base."

"Wouldn't he have told you?"

"Unless Carstairs convinced him not to inform me."

Cassiopia shook her head. He didn't blame her. It seemed far-fetched to him as well, but not impossible. Carstairs had left the base during her father's unaccounted hours and returned before suffering his fatal heart attack. No one knew where he'd gone or why.

"If Beacher did find the missing vials, would he give them to you to hold instead of telling you and calling in the authorities?"

Gabe had been asking himself the same question.

"I don't know," he admitted. "Locating the toxin wouldn't be enough. Beacher would want to prove who was behind the theft and why."

She chewed on her lower lip. "Because otherwise you both still looked guilty?"

"Yes."

"He could have been," she added softly.

He knew she saw his anger. "No."

"Let's not go back to one-syllable responses. He was your friend. You trust him. I got that. Let's say you're right—"

"How do you know he found anything?" Gabe interrupted. "The package he gave me could contain anything."

"Neither of us believes that. Why all this sudden interest in the toxin?"

Gabe snorted, "There's no sudden interest. Everyone has been looking for answers since the day it disappeared."

"But no one broke into my apartment or started killing people until now."

Gabe was tempted to contradict her, but these incidents must mean Beacher had become a threat to someone.

"Were you romantically involved with him?"

Her head jerked up. "No!"

"Beacher was drawn to attractive women."

"I suspect there's a compliment in there somewhere, but Beacher and I were not *involved.*" Ruefully, she added, "He tried that approach early on."

Gabe nearly smiled at the annoyed censure in her voice. Beacher had probably come away with scorch marks.

"Besides, according to the radio, he actually was engaged."

His amusement dissolved. "No."

She hesitated. "Andrea Fielding was *your* former fiancée, wasn't she?"

"Yes."

"The radio said she was his fiancée."

He shook his head. "No way. Beacher never liked Andrea. The dislike was mutual."

"Well, she must have told someone they were engaged or else where did the rumor come from?" Her eyes widened. "That's why you thought my attacker might have been a woman."

"Andrea was Dr. Pheng's lab assistant."

"That's right!" Her excitement mounted. "Do you think she was behind the theft?"

It was a possibility he and Beacher had discussed many times. "Andrea is impulsive. She came under intense scrutiny due to her position and her relationship with me. She could have been involved, but she couldn't have planned something like this and there's never been a shred of proof against her or anyone else."

"But do *you* think she was involved?"

"I don't know," he hedged. "I wouldn't rule it out." She'd been quick enough to distance herself from him after it went down. "Why do you think Beacher found the toxin?"

Cassiopia set down her glass but didn't release it. "Because I think I told him where to look."

"What?"

"Beacher's a hard person to ignore. I mean, he was."

This wasn't the first time she'd referred to him in the present tense. Gabe still did it himself, but if she'd killed Beacher or been involved in his murder, she wouldn't have any trouble thinking of him in the past tense.

"When I finally agreed to talk to him, Beacher asked me all sorts of questions about my dad. What he liked to do, places he liked to go. You know Dad clocked out early that day. There's a two-hour window that can't be accounted for. Everyone assumes he passed the vials to someone during that time frame."

"Me."

"Yes. But Beacher felt he'd passed off fakes instead and hid the real toxin and research."

"I know. We discussed it." That had been Beacher's favorite theory.

"Yes, but all your assumptions were based on my dad taking the stuff from the lab. What if he didn't? What if the toxin never left the lab?"

Immediately, Gabe shook his head. "Investigators turned that place inside out."

"I know, but—"

"If you're thinking your father switched the toxin with something else, he didn't. They checked everything he had access to and things he didn't. *Someone* would have found the toxin or the hard drive by now."

"True—if they'd stayed in the lab itself. But the facility was adding a wing back then. Dad used to go down to the new gym on his lunch hour and watch them work. When I mentioned that to Beacher, he got this stunned expression."

"No. We talked about that new wing," he refuted. "Every stone, every person working at that construction site was checked and double-checked."

"Right. But did they search the gym?"

Gabe gaped at her.

"Beacher asked me if Dad went to the construction area for any reason. I didn't know. He never mentioned it. Then he asked me what else Dad liked to do on his lunch hour, who he ate with, what sort of exercise equipment he liked best, things no one else has ever asked about."

Why hadn't Beacher mentioned this? Gabe ran his finger up and down the side of his glass of melting ice.

Tempering his rising excitement was difficult. This was the first new lead they'd had in years. Why hadn't Beacher said something?

"That building was searched thoroughly," he told her, thinking it through.

"Sure, but the gym? How much time would anyone spend in there? I mean, where would you hide something in a room full of machines that people use every day?"

"Precisely. Even if your father found a hiding place in there, would he take such a chance?"

Cassiopia shook her head. "I don't know. I never wanted to believe he took the stuff from the secured area in the first place. I can only tell you Beacher thought I'd hit on something."

"So do I," he agreed carefully. "At least, it's an angle no one else ever considered."

"That's why we need to know what's in that package he gave you."

"Yes."

Gabe could find Rochelle and make her let them into the gallery even at this hour. But his original argument still held. The last thing he wanted was to draw attention to the package.

"We can't get it until tomorrow."

"Why not? Where is it?"

Gabe saw no harm in telling her at this point. "Inside one of my pieces at a gallery in Olde Towne, Alexandria."

It was Cassiopia's turn to gape. Embarrassed, he gave a diffident shrug. "They're showcasing my work tomorrow."

"I was afraid all your work was destroyed in the explosion."

He thought with regret of the rosebush and chipmunks. Maybe the kiln had protected the piece. It hardly mattered now.

"I can't believe you hid something like that in one of your sculptures! Are you out of your mind? What if someone finds it?"

He ran a hand tiredly over his jaw. "For one thing, we don't know what Beacher found and, for another, it isn't in the sculpture itself. There's a concealed drawer in the base."

And just in case something happened to him before they got it, someone needed to know where the package was.

"Why would you give it to the gallery?"

Gabe sighed. He was more tired than he wanted to admit. "I didn't. Rochelle wanted both pieces for the show. She kept me distracted while her men took them out to the van."

"Who is Rochelle? Could she be after the toxin?"

Gabe didn't even have to consider that. "No."

"Then why would she take something without permission?"

"She wanted the large pair of lions to be the centerpiece of the exhibition. I only agreed to exhibit one, but Rochelle likes to have her own way." He curbed his annoyance.

Cassiopia brooded over that. "I guess it's just as well. Otherwise the toxin might have exploded along with your house. But why would anyone blow up your house?"

"Good question. First thing tomorrow morning I'll go and—"

"*We'll* go. What gallery?"

He thought about arguing, but it wasn't worth it at this point and there was no reason not to tell her. "First Impressions."

"I've heard of it."

Cassiopia covered a yawn. Gabe noticed the lines of fatigue on her face. He felt the pull himself.

"We should get some rest. We need to be up and moving early."

Her glance flew to the bed and back to him.

"I said rest, not sex." Even if she was the first woman since his accident to stir his libido.

She met his gaze squarely with a hint of humor. "So blowing up the house wasn't just a ploy to get me into bed?"

He could learn to like this woman and her tart tongue. "Maybe next time."

Her expression went from playful to serious again. "How did you know to rush us out of there tonight?"

"I didn't." Gabe rolled his shoulders, which were tight with renewed tension. Fatigue was making him sluggish. "The house was being watched, Cassiopia. When you showed up it seemed prudent to get you out of there right away. I suspected Sliffman was coming back with a search warrant. Whoever he left on surveillance must have seen you climbing through my window."

"Oh." She pushed at a strand of hair. "So who blew it up?"

"I don't know. We'll try to find out tomorrow."

"Okay." Cassiopia stood abruptly. "Which side of the bed do you want?"

She wasn't as indifferent as she wanted him to

believe. That pleased him. If things had been different he might have enjoyed getting her into bed for an entirely different reason.

"Take your pick," he offered.

"This side."

That would put him closer to the door, which was all to the good. If someone came in, they'd have to go through him first.

"Sleep under the covers," he told her, "I'll stay on top."

"That isn't necessary. I trust you."

He raised his eyebrows.

"With my virtue," she amended. "I know you aren't interested in me *that* way."

He stood slowly. Deliberately he let his gaze sweep over her body. "You know nothing at all."

Her lips parted on a silent *oh* of surprise. The pink deepened to red. He didn't know what had prompted him, but he regretted the impulse immediately.

"I told you before, I'm not a rapist, Cassiopia."

"I haven't forgotten. And I'm sure you haven't forgotten I shot at my last attacker."

His eyes crinkled. "You did mention you're a terrible shot."

"Not at close range."

He let his lips curve then. "Truce."

"Absolutely. You should smile more often. You're really not bad-looking when you aren't hiding behind your scar and that glare. I'll use the bathroom first."

Astounded, Gabe watched her stride into the bathroom and close the door. Cassiopia was one surprise after another. Too bad they hadn't met five or six years ago. Except she'd have been too young for him to notice back then.

She wasn't too young now. Good thing he was scarred and jaded. This looked as if it were going to be a long night.

Chapter Seven

Cassy hadn't expected to fall asleep almost the minute she closed her eyes, but she never heard Gabriel come to bed. It was disconcerting to wake and find him watching her from the opposite side of the bed.

His expression was curious, almost tender. He looked years younger with his features relaxed like that. Without thought, she reached out and lightly touched his scar. Instantly, the mask was in place. He rolled off the bed with feline grace.

"Are you one of those people who wake up quick or slow?" he demanded.

She sat up, cursing her stupidity and his manly sensitivity. "When there's a man in my bed, I wake up fast."

Humor touched his eyes. "I think anything I say to that will simply get me in trouble."

"Smart man."

"We need to get moving."

"What time is it?" But she'd already spotted the bedside clock.

"Six thirty-four."

"You've got eyes in the back of your head?"

"Looked at my watch a second ago. You want the bathroom first?"

"Yes." She scrambled out of bed and hurried to the bathroom door, where she paused.

"You know, your scars aren't nearly as off-putting as you'd like to believe." And she stepped inside and closed the door before he could respond.

Showering was probably fruitless since she'd have to put her dirty clothes back on for the third day in a row, but she needed to feel her skin was clean at least.

The events of yesterday had taken on a nightmarish quality of unreality. It suddenly struck her that neither one of them had a home to return to now. She was angry and sad over the loss of a few irreplaceable treasures, but Gabriel had lost far more. She tried hard not to think about Beacher.

Gabriel was a thoughtful male. Not only had he let her use the facilities first, the toilet seat was down and the room was tidy. Although she hadn't heard him, he must have taken a shower last night. Damp towels had been folded neatly and stacked. The tub and shower had been wiped down. The military had left more marks on him than scars and a shattered life. It pained Cassy to think she'd spent so many years hating the wrong man.

The thought stopped her. When had she decided for sure that Gabriel was innocent? Beacher had opened her mind to the possibility, but she couldn't point to any one thing as the defining moment. Still, somewhere along the way the lion image had taken hold and she'd begun to view him as a trapped beast, caged by forces beyond his control.

In a few hours they could be in possession of a

deadly toxin that could wipe out thousands. It was a chillingly sober thought.

Once again the bedroom was empty when she emerged. This time she scanned the room until she spotted his helmet on a chair. She opened the door when she heard the card key in the lock. Gabriel held a tray with steaming cups, breakfast rolls and fruit.

"A woman could get used to this, you know."

His eyebrows arched. There was a flash that was definitely humor in those soft brown eyes.

One cup held hot water, the second coffee. A third cup contained orange juice. Cassy reached for the thick black brew as soon as he set the tray down. Taking a careful sip she let the caffeine seep into her bloodstream.

His lips quirked. He added a tea bag to the second cup and carried it with him into the bathroom. "I'll be ready as soon as I shave."

"With what? A pocketknife?"

"They had disposable razors at the desk."

"Ouch. Aren't you going to eat something?"

"I had oatmeal and juice while you were in the shower."

Of course he had. She almost asked how he'd known she hadn't wanted oatmeal as well, then shuddered at the thought and selected a cream-cheese-and-raspberry Danish. Gabriel closed the bathroom door.

After the toilet flushed she called out to him. "What time does this gallery open?"

Gabriel opened the door. "I've no idea, but I want to be there when Rochelle arrives."

"She's the owner?"

"Yes."

Unselfconsciously, he lathered his face from a tiny

shaving can and opened the packaged razor. Cassy knew she should move away, but she watched with genuine curiosity as the blade carved a swath through the foam. She'd never watched a man shave before, but having nicked her legs often enough she was impressed, even if it did feel uncomfortably intimate.

"Any chance we can pick up some clean clothing first?"

"At this hour?"

He had a point.

"See if you can find a newscast," he suggested.

"Sure. I'd rather not be standing here when you slice yourself with that thing."

The words reminded her of Beacher's throat gaping like a second smile. Queasy enough to lose the Danish she turned away, thankful for something to take her mind from that image. She located the television remote. A local station actually carried news at this ungodly hour and she settled in the chair with her coffee, halfheartedly listening to the troubles of the world. Minutes later, she was jerked out of her complacency when a blazing house came on-screen.

"Recapping our top stories this morning, an explosion inside a house in Frederick, Maryland, took the life of an unidentified man late last night. Police are not saying—"

"Gabriel!"

"—what caused the blast—"

He appeared silently beside her as a camera panned over the remains of his house.

"—that brought neighbors pouring from their homes in this quiet suburban community, but a possible gas leak has not been ruled out. A three-car pileup on the inner loop of the Beltway has left…"

She rounded on him. "I thought we were alone!"

"So did I."

He wiped the remaining traces of foam from his face with a towel and strode back to the bathroom. Cassy hurried after him.

"Then who was killed?"

"Did you notice the two men standing off to one side when the camera panned across the scene? The tall one was Len Sliffman with Homeland Security."

Her stomach gave a lurch. "I remember him."

"The one in uniform was Major Bruce Huntington."

She hadn't noticed either man but both identifications chilled her. There had been a Captain Huntington who'd had something to do with base security four years ago. She didn't think she'd ever spoken with him.

"We didn't turn on any lights in the house last night," he pointed out. "I suspect whoever was watching came to investigate after you climbed through the window. He must have set off the explosion."

"I don't understand. You mean he planted the explosives?"

"No."

"Then why did the house blow up?"

"There are a couple of possibilities. The most obvious is that someone planted claymores on a trip wire on the stairs or inside my bedroom door."

"Claymores?"

"An explosive device. It could have been something else on a detonator, but the trip wire is the most likely. They couldn't be sure when I'd go upstairs and I doubt anyone stuck around to set it off manually."

Cassy shuddered. "How can you say such things so calmly? Why would someone try to kill you?"

"My winning personality? Grab the helmet."

"Gabriel!"

There was no trace of humor in his voice or on his face as he shook his head. "I don't know who or why, Cassiopia. I'm still trying to work through all the ramifications."

His icy tone churned her stomach.

"We need to go. Now. By now they know the body isn't mine. Guess who'll be the number-one suspect."

CASSY REALIZED HE WAS RIGHT. The authorities probably would believe Gabriel had planted the explosives. Hadn't that been her first thought as well?

"Do you have everything?"

She grabbed the jacket she'd draped over one of the chairs and nodded.

"I was out of the house for hours yesterday. Plenty of time for someone to rig the explosives."

Gabe led her to the back entrance they'd used the night before. He slowed his pace as he realized she was practically running to keep up with his longer stride.

"As far as I know, you're the only person who ever disliked me enough to want me dead and I doubt you have the skill to rig an explosion."

"That's not funny!"

"Agreed. Put the helmet on."

"Wait!" She grabbed his arm, jerking him to a halt when he would have mounted the bike.

"Who was killed?"

Gabe shrugged. "Whoever Sliffman had watching the house. I'm guessing someone inexperienced. I doubt he was told to go inside and he should have been watching for traps when he did. Your arrival probably saved my life. I doubt I'd have been watching for a trip wire, either, when I went upstairs."

Her expression was so stricken Gabe didn't stop to think. He tilted her chin and kissed her on the mouth. It wasn't a gentle peck.

For a moment she was rigid in his arms, then she softened, pressing her body into his and returning the kiss in full measure.

He'd wondered what it would be like to taste her, but he hadn't anticipated the wild hunger that raced through his body. He found himself responding greedily to her small sounds of pleasure.

She started to fling her arms around his neck and clunked him in the head with the forgotten helmet.

"Ow!"

"Sorry." She swayed when he pulled back to rub his head.

"All you had to do was ask me to stop."

"No! I didn't mean…"

She hesitated, seemed to realize he was teasing and glared at him.

He wanted her, but he didn't want to want her. She confused him, but he hadn't wanted that kiss to end. He didn't think she had, either. She was unlike anyone he'd ever known. But while she might want to trust him, she didn't. Not really.

"Let's go."

He took the helmet from her hand and set it on her head. Cover temptation. This was no time for the crazy sort of thoughts he was having. On the other hand, he'd wanted to create a diversion for her thoughts and it appeared he'd been successful.

He helped her onto the bike, aware of the wobbly arms she slid lightly around his waist.

He wasn't sure he wanted to know what she was thinking. Cassiopia was the first woman he'd touched in almost four years. How ironic that she still couldn't be sure he hadn't killed her father.

Always nice to know his timing still sucked.

It started to rain before they cleared the parking lot. As omens went, this seemed par for the course. If he'd been home, Gabe would have left the bike and taken the truck. Motorcycles and rain were a dangerous combination.

Gabe swore to himself as he steered them toward the highway. Wind slapped rain into his eyes. He lowered his gaze and the rear tire lost traction. They started to slide on the oil coming to the surface of the road. Gabe dropped his speed even further. Rain began falling more quickly. This wasn't going to work. He couldn't see without his helmet. He'd have to pull over.

No sooner did he have that thought than a pair of deer broke from the trees and darted in front of him. If they'd kept moving it would have been no problem, but they came to a startled stop.

Gabe braked hard and swerved. The bike began to hydroplane. Cassiopia gripped his waist tightly as the bike did a slow slide sideways across the road before spinning completely around.

Gabe struggled to keep them upright and steer into the slide. He thought they'd make it until the back tire reached the slick, wet grass. Even before they plunged into the trees and went down, he knew he'd lost the battle.

"GABRIEL! GABRIEL! Don't you dare die on me!"

Gabe opened his eyes and shut them against the rain and the blurry figure bending over him.

"You all right, lady?"

A stranger's voice. Male and young.

"Help me get this bike off him."

Cassiopia moved out of his line of sight to give orders and a sudden rush of memories swamped him.

A car pulling into a garage in front of him. An explosion. A wall of fire. A second explosion. Pain.

He blinked uncomprehendingly at the trees overhead. Moisture drenched him. Why was it raining? It hadn't been raining.

"Ready? Lift!"

His thoughts cleared. His bike had gone down on the side of the road. They'd missed the trees somehow, but his leg was trapped. The pressure eased as the bike was lifted. Gabe jerked free, scraping skin in the process. Cassiopia gave a soft cry. The bike landed with a thud beside him.

"What's wrong?" the stranger demanded. "Are you hurt?"

"My wrist," Cassiopia replied. "I think it's broken. I must have landed on it."

Gabe struggled to get to his feet. Strong hands reached out to help.

"An' I had to go an' forget my cell phone this morning. If you all have one I'll call for an ambulance."

"No," Gabe told his rescuer. The last thing he wanted was the police and an ambulance. "Cassiopia?"

"You're bleeding."

He touched the back of his head. Warm blood

mingled with the rain. A lump was swelling around the cut. He shut his eyes against a sudden wave of dizziness.

"Gabriel!"

Probably a concussion, he decided as his stomach gave an uneasy lurch. His leg began to throb.

"Easy, man. Lean on me."

"Is he all right? Gabriel, are you—"

"Give me a minute."

"I saw what happened," the stranger was saying. "That was some driving, man. I can't believe you missed all them trees. I can flag down another car and get someone to call an ambulance, but it might be quicker if I just drive you to the hospital. We'll have to leave the bike."

Gabe glanced at his motorcycle. Nothing appeared too badly damaged, but he couldn't tell for sure. Cassiopia pressed her left arm against her middle in obvious pain. His helmet dangled forgotten in her other hand. She looked to be in shock. Even if the bike was okay, she wouldn't be riding it anymore this morning.

"Do you have one of those twenty-four-hour, walk-in emergency clinics nearby?"

Going to a hospital was too risky. He'd just as soon not answer official questions. There was no doubt in his mind that Huntington would believe Gabe had set the trip wire.

Would a walk-in clinic feel compelled to report this accident? Probably not. They should be able to get Cassiopia's wrist x-rayed and get away before anyone official discovered where they were.

"I think there's a walk-in place over on Talbert," their rescuer offered after a moment's thought, "but are you sure you wouldn't rather go to the hospital? I don't know what all a small place like that can do."

"It'll be fine. Mind giving us a lift?"

"No problem, man. Can you make it to my car?"

"Yes." One way or another.

"Those deer are a menace," the man continued.

"They probably feel the same way about us," Cassiopia told him as they started for the road.

While there was pain in her voice, it sounded stronger. She'd cope. He wasn't so sure about him.

Gabe collapsed gratefully onto the front passenger seat of the small sedan that waited on the shoulder of the road. His vision was a little blurred, but the deer, he noticed, had made good their escape.

If he'd been alone, he'd have tried to get the bike back on the road despite his leg and his headache, but he couldn't do it with Cassiopia in pain. He shut his eyes. The world was taking on a bad tendency to tilt and spin. His head throbbed in cadence with the windshield wipers.

"Gabriel, wake up! Stay with us!"

He jerked his eyes open. "'M 'wake."

"Can you hurry?" Cassiopia demanded, leaning over the backseat. She touched his face gently. He wanted to flinch away but it would take too much effort. Besides, part of him wanted to nestle into that hand and savor her touch.

"Not unless you want to end up in the trees again," the driver was saying. "It's coming down so hard I can barely see the road."

A streak of brilliant light was accompanied by the crash of thunder. Gabe tuned it out. It would have been nice to succumb to the inviting well of deep gray that waited whenever he closed his eyes, but Cassiopia's gentle touch prevented it. Passing out would be bad. He had to stay alert.

Gabe roused more fully when their rescuer pulled into a small shopping center. Cassiopia pointed out they'd already made him late for work when the man offered to accompany them inside. She thanked him while Gabe stiffly maneuvered himself out of the car.

He swayed unsteadily. Cassiopia appeared at his side.

"Lean on me."

"'M okay."

"Sure you are. You're a tough guy. Guys always think they're all right. It isn't macho to be in pain. Hopefully if you don't bleed to death you'll be fine."

"Head wounds always bleed."

"There's blood running down your ripped pants, too."

A glance at his upper thigh showed a gash beneath the torn fabric. Now that she'd pointed it out, new pain vied with his throbbing head for attention.

"Just a cut," he told her as they stepped inside what was nothing more than a storefront. "How's your wrist?"

"It's felt better."

The small clinic was bustling despite the early hour. Somewhere out of sight a small child wailed loudly. The keening sound drove splinters of knife-edged pain into his skull.

Gabe decided giving the busy woman at the front desk a phony name would needlessly arouse suspicions. These people were too busy to worry about a pair of fools who'd driven their motorcycle off the side of the road.

The wait was long, but finally a stressed young doctor confirmed Gabe's concussion. X-rays determined nothing else was broken despite considerable bruising, but both his head wound and the cut on his leg required stitches.

Stoically, Gabe allowed them to shave a section of hair on the back of his head in order to stitch the wound closed. Given his looks, he figured another scar or two didn't matter. What he really needed was the ibuprofen they finally gave him for his throbbing headache.

Cassiopia's injuries proved less serious. Besides minor cuts and bruises, her wrist was sprained, though thankfully, not broken. They iced it down, wrapped it and put her arm in a sling, while the small clinic continued to fill past capacity.

"It's always like this when it rains," he heard his nurse grumble to the doctor.

The thunderstorm had passed and the rain had slowed to a steady drizzle by the time they finally limped outside looking the worse for wear. Gabe gazed around the small shopping center and realized they were stranded.

"Do you know how to get back to the bike?"

Cassiopia's expression stated clearly she felt he'd lost his mind. "I wasn't paying attention, but you aren't going to ride it now. You look like you can barely walk."

"Thanks."

"Besides, I wouldn't get back on that motorcycle if I did know where it was. And don't you dare tell me it's like falling off a horse. I wouldn't get back on one of them, either."

His lips twitched.

"We could call for a taxi," she suggested.

"On a Friday? In this rain? We'd be lucky to see one in two hours."

"Okay. Good point. There's a pancake place across the street. We could go there and wait while we figure out what to do."

"Not a bad idea." Except the thought of food made his stomach roll.

"Yeah, except we're covered in mud and blood and grass. Unless you want everyone staring at us, I suggest we stop in there first."

He followed her pointing finger to *there.* A discreet little sign several doors down read New Again. The small, mom-and-pop store apparently sold used everything, from clothing to furniture.

Gabe didn't have to glance at his torn, bloodstained pants to know he made a bedraggled picture. He tried not to limp as they walked beneath the awning to the store's front door.

They'd lost so much time inside the clinic it was far too late to beat Rochelle and her crew to the gallery. She hadn't tried calling his cell phone yet, so she'd probably seen the news about his house. Since they hadn't identified the victim, odds were she believed he was dead.

Two middle-aged women eyed them nervously as they entered the cluttered shop. Gabe left it to Cassiopia to explain their battered condition. The pair tsked like mother hens over her while giving *him* plenty of space. That didn't stop them from making pointed remarks about the dangers of motorcycles. Gabe concentrated on the clothing for sale.

Mindful of the stitches in the back of his head, he located a ball cap to cover his shaved scalp. After a bit of a search he found a pair of dark jeans and a navy shirt in his size. At the last second he spotted a plain navy sweatshirt and carried everything into the make-shift dressing room. Curtains enclosed the space rather than walls.

Deciding everything fit well enough, he used his old shirt to wipe down his jacket as best he could, then stepped outside to hand his torn and stained items to one of the women. Reluctantly, she agreed to pitch them in the trash.

Cassiopia had been gazing at a rack of inexpensive earrings while waiting her turn. A pair of crystal earrings and a matching pendant caught his eye as she carried her bundle into the claustrophobic space. The crystals were shaped to resemble small roses. As he lifted them, the bits of glass reflected the overhead lights.

Questioning his sanity, Gabe paid for them while one of the women helped Cassiopia. Belatedly, he realized it would be difficult for her to use her left arm.

Gabe brooded, gazing around the shop. There were some interesting items for sale. The small painting of a lion captured his attention. He was staring at it when Cassiopia joined him a few minutes later. She'd selected a pair of jeans similar to his, a white blouse and a bright red sweater.

"I like it," she told him. "Good use of color. He sort of reminds me of you with that fierce expression."

"Thanks."

"Don't mention it. Going to buy it?"

"No walls left."

He was sorry for his flip remark when her teasing expression faded instantly.

"You all set?"

"Yes," she agreed.

He strode to the counter, but Cassiopia insisted on paying for her own purchases. Rather than make a fuss, he walked to the door and stared out at the main road. Was it going to rain all day?

"Ready?" she asked, coming up beside him.

"Yes. Here." He handed her the jewelry.

"What's this?"

Gabe shrugged, aware of their interested audience.

"They reminded me of you."

He wasn't sure why he'd done it. He'd never bought a woman a present without a reason before and it felt foolish. She probably wouldn't even like them.

Her lips parted in surprise and her eyes glittered. Gabe hustled her out of the store, but she stopped him outside by laying a hand on his arm.

"Gabriel."

He was startled when she reached up and kissed him lightly.

"Thank you."

He looked away. He'd never been uncomfortable around a woman before. Certainly not when one had kissed him, but then, his face hadn't resembled a Halloween mask the last time it had happened.

"Let me take those," he demanded gruffly.

Those consisted of a bulky shopping bag with her old clothing and some other stuff she must have purchased, including an umbrella.

"Wait. Help me put these on first," she requested, holding out the bits of glass.

It felt intimate, not to mention awkward, sliding the

earrings into the small holes in her dainty earlobes. Just as bad was circling her neck with the delicate chain. Lovers did things like this, not virtual strangers.

"Thank you."

He didn't meet her eyes as he inclined his head. "Hungry?"

"You're supposed to say, you're welcome."

He set his teeth. "You're welcome."

Cassiopia opened the umbrella. A tiny smile played on her lips. "I could eat."

He doubted he could.

The restaurant across the street was conspicuously uncrowded given the hour. It should have bustled with a lunch crowd, but they quickly realized their waitress was more interested in flirting with her coworker than in her two ragtag customers. No doubt that accounted for all the empty places. They settled into a booth, finally ordered and sat back.

"Smile. You'll scare the cook."

"He can't see me." But Gabe felt himself start to relax. "You realize we'll probably get ptomaine in here."

Cassiopia grinned. "I'm hungry enough to risk it. You look different in that cap. Younger. How's your head?"

"Fine."

She made a face. "Right. Why'd I ask? I'm sure it hurts as much as my wrist."

"Sorry."

"Forget it. The accident wasn't your fault. I'd have been more upset if you'd hit those deer. I have something to give you, too."

While her words startled him, he knew what it was even before he looked inside the bag he'd carried for her. How she'd bought it without him noticing he wasn't sure, but he didn't need to unwrap the small package to know it was the lion painting.

His chest tightened painfully. She'd bought this for him. For no reason. He didn't know what to say. No woman had ever given him a gift before.

"For when you get new walls."

Discomfited, he shook his head. "You shouldn't have done that."

"Neither should you, but I really like these crystals." And then with her usual bluntness she added, "Why is this so awkward?"

"I don't know. Do you always say what you think?"

"Most of the time. You should try it. It saves misunderstandings. What are we going to do now?"

Relieved by her change of topic he nodded toward the waitress bearing plates. "Eat."

CASSY MADE A FACE at him, but was secretly as relieved by the interruption as Gabriel appeared to be. The painting had been a spur-of-the-moment decision. She hadn't known he'd bought the jewelry, but there'd been something almost wistful in his expression when he'd looked at that painting. She had a feeling few people had ever given Gabriel gifts, particularly in the last few years. Beacher had said his parents were deceased and he wasn't close to any other family he might have. She knew he had few friends, if any, and it saddened her.

"Lowe is German for lion," he told her.

Her pulse quickened. It was the first time he'd initiated a casual conversation. And the name fit him so perfectly.

"Is that where your ancestors are from? Germany?"

"On my father's side anyway."

"Where did the Gabriel come from?"

"My mother. She liked the sound of it. You're the only one beside her who's ever called me Gabriel. Most people call me Gabe."

"And most people call me Cassy."

His expression lightened with definite humor. "Cassiopia sounds nicer."

"So does Gabriel."

The smile was rueful, but it was still a smile. "Truce?"

"Truce," she agreed. "Now what?"

"We need a car."

The man was exasperating. "I just happen to have one. Unfortunately, it's parked two blocks from your house."

"Too dangerous. The police have probably found it by now."

Cassy set down her fork, no longer interested in food as she thought about the dead man in his house.

"We should go to the authorities."

He lowered his voice even though the last couple seated closest to them had just left. "They'll believe I set that explosive."

"But you didn't!"

"Prove it."

His flat tone was chilling. A shiver moved down her spine. "You can't prove a negative."

He inclined his head, lifted his fork and continued eating. He'd been trying to do just that for the past four years, she realized.

Cassy reached for her coffee to give her shaking hands something to do. Sipping at the bitter brew she tried to think past the creeping fear.

"I could call a friend to lend us a car."

"No. Too dangerous."

"Why would anyone be watching my friends?"

Gabriel simply shook his head and continued to eat mechanically. She was almost certain he didn't taste his food.

"The gallery is open by now," he pointed out between bites. "We can't afford to draw attention to it."

"I could create a distraction."

"No doubt. Then what?"

"What do you mean?"

"If the package contains what we think it does, what do we do with it?"

"Turn it over to… Surely they won't think…" The coffee did a lurch and roll in her stomach. Of course the authorities would think Gabriel had had the vials all along. A few weeks ago she would have thought the same thing.

He set down his fork. "Do you know how to handle the toxin if we find it?"

"You don't handle it. If even a drop of that stuff gets spilled we could have a disaster. Of course, we wouldn't live long enough to bear witness. And what if someone else already found the package?"

"We'd know by now."

For the first time, she saw vulnerability in his expression. For all his take-charge, macho attitude, Gabriel was scared, too.

"We have to do something."

He stared out the window. Suddenly, his expression brightened. "I know how to get a car. We'll buy one."

"Of course. How simple. Why didn't I think of that? We'll just buy one. You've got deeper pockets than I do."

His lips curved. "Not so deep, but we don't need to ride in style. There's a used-car lot right down the street."

"You're just going to march over there and buy a car."

"Not on this leg," he agreed, "but I can limp."

"You're serious."

"Watch me."

Chapter Eight

Gabe found the cheapest car on the lot and made a ridiculous offer. The resulting transaction took longer than Cassy would have thought, given they were paying cash, but eventually they climbed inside a small white sedan that had seen better days.

"Are you sure this thing will run? Shouldn't we at least have given it a test drive?"

"It's been state inspected. It'll run."

"Gabriel, it's eleven years old!"

"That's why we got it so cheap."

"Cheap? I wouldn't have given him five dollars. Did you see how much mileage it has on it? And look at this interior! It's in horrible shape."

"It's transportation."

"Only if it runs! You're crazy, you know that, right?"

"Sanity's overrated."

His rakish grin stopped her mid-rant. The man had a killer grin. He'd be devilishly appealing if he set his mind to it. And this was not the time to be thinking how attractive he was.

"How is it you have an envelope stuffed with hundred-dollar bills anyhow?"

She'd seen him pull the envelope from the box of cereal herself, but her mind had been on other things at the time. Gabe started the engine and Cassy quickly reached for her seat belt.

"I set money aside for emergencies. I think this qualifies, don't you?"

Without being told, she knew the emergency he'd expected was being arrested and charged. He would not appreciate her pity.

Rain had begun again. The windshield wipers squealed in protest as they sluggishly swiped at the glass.

"You aren't really going to take this thing on the highway, are you?"

"Would you rather stop and pick up my bike?"

He'd do it, too. "No. What are you going to do about your motorcycle?"

"We'll go back for it later."

Not if she had anything to say. "Someone might steal it."

"Then I'll report it missing."

Cassy sat back and didn't say another word until they were in Olde Towne, Alexandria. She stared out at the small shops as they drove down the busy streets.

"Hey! Wasn't that the art gallery you just passed? First Impressions?"

"Yes."

He continued driving.

"Where are you going?"

"Sliffman and Huntington were going inside."

Cassy inhaled sharply. "You saw them? Do you think they'll find the package?"

"We can only hope."

Her lips parted in astonishment. "You *want* them to find that package?"

As they came to a red traffic signal, Gabriel twisted to look at her. "I *want* that stuff back where it belongs. I'd *like* to see it destroyed along with all research of that type. But then, I'd like a perfect world, too."

As he faced forward again and started into the intersection, Cassy tried to get her mind around an entirely new assessment of Gabriel Lowe.

"I never pictured you as an environmentalist," she ventured. "I mean, being former military and all."

"My lawyer arranged for the military service to keep me out of jail."

Cassy forced her gaping mouth shut. His expression was sardonic.

"A pair of buddies and I got drunk one night. One of them decided to get even with a rival who'd made a move on his girl. Unfortunately, we were so wasted he picked the wrong house."

"What did you do?"

"Actually, I don't remember doing anything besides throwing up, but I was there when the cops arrived to find them smashing in the windshield of a car. The three of us were arrested. Since I had good grades and had been in ROTC, someone pulled strings. I was told I had leadership potential if I could lose the attitude." He gave another shrug. "You can see how well that worked out."

Cassy was torn between amusement and shock. "What did you want to be?" she asked after a moment.

"Good at something."

"You are," she told him softly, thinking of his incredible sculptures. "Why don't we just park and wait for them to leave?"

"Odds are they'll have someone stick around to keep an eye on the place. We'll come back."

"Okay. What are we going to do instead?"

"I'm going to drop you somewhere while I go and have a talk with…an old friend."

"Andrea Fielding?"

He shot her a startled glance and she shrugged.

"It was either that or Dr. Pheng and somehow I don't think the two of you were ever buds."

"You're sharp."

"Thank you, but the possibilities seemed limited. I know everyone's been investigated up one side and down the other, but the media is saying Andrea was Beacher's fiancée and we both know she wasn't."

"Very sharp."

It didn't sound like a compliment.

"That's why I'm sticking with you. Two heads and all that, remember? And don't remind me they're playing for keeps. I'm one of the people they're playing with. I'll feel a whole lot safer next to you."

"Why?"

"Because I trust you."

Gabe jerked as if he'd been sucker punched. Good, he needed a few jolts if that's what it took him to see he wasn't alone. He was a scary person on several levels, but he was no killer. Hard to believe she'd ever thought differently.

The legal system might not have placed a physical prison around him, but Gabriel had been tried, convicted and sentenced in the eyes of the public. He'd been in solitary confinement a long time now and like any other trapped beast he wouldn't trust easily. That was okay. Cassy had learned the need for some patience while waiting for a desired result.

"Do you know where Andrea lives?" she asked.

"I know. It would be best if I drop you off somewhere."

"Maybe from your perspective, but that isn't going to happen. You're stuck with me."

A muscle twitched in his jaw. "Are you always this obstinate?"

"Pretty much."

Cassy expected an argument but he didn't say anything more. She wasn't surprised that he knew where Andrea lived. She'd be willing to bet he could find everyone connected with the events of four years ago.

They drove back into Maryland, where he did surprise her when he pulled off the interstate in Montgomery County instead of continuing on to Frederick.

"It's Friday," Gabriel explained even though she hadn't asked. "She'll be at work."

Where Cassy should be at the moment. She hadn't given work a thought. She should have called in sick, but it was too late now. She'd have to come up with a story on Monday. The thought made her cringe, but at least her boss was taking a long weekend. No one should be looking for her.

"Doesn't Andrea still work at the base?"

"No. She took a position with a private lab that does genetic research. I don't see her car." He slowly cruised the parking lot of a low brick building.

"Late lunch?"

"Very late."

"Maybe she rode in with someone else today. Or she could have left early."

As he pulled into a visitor's spot Cassy laid a hand on his wrist and felt his tension. He was far from the calm he projected. "Why don't you let me ask for her? If she hears your name, she might not talk to us."

"Good thinking."

The cheerful receptionist told them Andrea hadn't come in today.

"Now what?" Cassy asked as they climbed back in the car.

"Her condo."

"You're worried."

"Things are coming to a head."

Cassy frowned. "That's good, isn't it?"

"Depends if we survive."

"You're so reassuring."

He didn't smile.

Andrea's condominium was in a nice, well-kept neighborhood that to Cassy's eyes looked rather pricey for a mere lab assistant. Gabe scanned the mostly empty parking area and pulled in beside a late model sporty-looking red car. Leaving their car running, he climbed out with a terse, "Wait here."

It took Cassy several seconds to realize the red car was occupied. Gabe favored his leg slightly as he hurried around to the driver's side where dark hair was the only visible sign of the person slumped over the steering wheel. Dread sent Cassy out of the car.

Gabe jerked the door open and stopped. He touched

the person lightly. They didn't twitch. The bleakness that stared from his eyes as he lifted his head froze Cassy in her tracks.

"Get back in the car."

Cassy obeyed without a word. Gabe shut the car door and used his jacket to wipe where his fingers had touched the metal. Fear speared cold talons down her spine.

An expensive looking SUV pulled into the lot and parked a few spaces away. The pair of young women who got out sent them a curious look from beneath a pair of brightly colored umbrellas.

This was the wrong neighborhood for a clunker like the one they were driving. And Gabriel, well, his forbidding expression gave Cassy chills.

"Andrea?" she asked as he got back inside the car.

"Her throat was slit from behind." His voice was utterly devoid of emotion.

Cassy began searching through her bag for her cell phone.

"What are you doing?"

"We need to call the police. Those women saw us. They're going to remember us. If we don't call, we're going to look guilty." She was surprised at how calm she sounded. She was shaking so bad she doubted she'd be able to punch in the number.

"I'll do it." He whipped his own cell phone from a pocket and dialed. "I want to report a suspicious death."

Calmly, he gave the dispatcher the location then hung up and put the car in reverse. The women had disappeared inside the building.

"She's been dead for hours," he told Cassy in that emotionless, stranger's voice. "Her killer must have waited in the backseat, yanked her head back by her hair and slit her throat before she could struggle."

"My God!" She pictured Beacher and wanted to throw up.

"I doubt she even marked him. It was a professional hit."

"What does that mean?"

"Her assailant knew how to kill. Military-trained, at a guess. There was no hesitation. Andrea must have been the inside person after all."

Cassy inhaled sharply. "What?"

"She was involved in the theft of the toxin."

And Andrea was the woman Gabriel once loved. Maybe he still did. He might be an expert at hiding his emotions, but that didn't mean he didn't have them. Cassy would never forget the bleakness in his eyes when he first looked up.

She rested a hand on his arm and felt the steel of bunched muscles. "I'm sorry."

He didn't respond, but he didn't shake off her hand, either. Cassy squeezed lightly and withdrew. Pain twisted her heart. Everyone he cared about was dead and she didn't know how to comfort him.

"Beacher always believed she was the one who stole Pheng's notes and the hard drives from the safe on the base. He kept trying, but she wouldn't talk to us. Recently we learned her brother died shortly after the toxin went missing."

Cassy frowned. "What does her brother's death have to do with anything?"

"Ron was very intense and very anti-military. He hated that Andrea worked on a military base. He and I didn't exactly hit it off, but I never saw much of him even though he lived with Andrea. Their parents were dead. Both were ex-military, and their dad died in a training accident."

"Accounting for Ron's dislike, huh? How did he die?"

"He fell from the top floor of a parking garage and broke his neck after leaving a popular D.C. club one night."

"Oh, geez."

"He was underage, but his blood alcohol level was well over the legal limit. There was no sign that he was pushed or forced over."

"You don't think it was an accident."

"It *could* have been an accident, but the timing bothered us."

He didn't take his eyes from the road. The rain was heavy again and the wipers were struggling to keep up. He reached for the defroster.

"Stupidity happens, Gabe. People do die. What makes you think there's a connection?"

He shrugged. "Beacher and I began looking at Ron's close friends. Before he died there was a core group that used to hang out at Andrea's house. It occurred to us to wonder if someone had convinced them they should show the world what the government was doing behind closed doors. They were all college kids, antiestablishment, pro-environment, typical dissident types. Teenage idealists are easily manipulated. That's why so many get caught up in cults."

"They were in a cult?"

"No, but they could have been manipulated."

"Into stealing the toxin?"

"Or helping someone else do it."

"That sounds pretty far-fetched."

Gabe nodded. "I believe I mentioned grasping at straws. We'd exhausted every other lead and to our surprise, it turned out Ron's girlfriend quit school immediately after he died and moved to Chicago."

"So?"

He shot her a quick glance. "She disappeared on her way to a job interview shortly after moving. She hasn't been seen since."

Cassy felt the start of goose bumps. "Do the authorities know about this?"

"Beacher has...*had* an inside source. Supposedly they took a hard look at Ron's death. Nothing came of the investigation but they also searched for the girlfriend. Don't forget the authorities already had a strong suspect."

Him. Her nails bit into her palms and she forced her fingers to relax before they drew blood.

"Everyone remotely connected with the toxin was put under a microscope, Cassiopia. Even you."

"So?" she prodded when he fell silent.

"All of those kids are dead."

Cassy was stunned. "That can't be a coincidence! You need to tell someone!"

"They know—" he smiled without humor "—but in their shoes, I'd still suspect me, too."

Cassy inhaled.

"I was engaged to Andrea. I knew her brother. And can you see your father responding to a threat from a group of college kids? I can't."

"Then what did they have to do with this?"

"You know how you said Beacher was hard to ignore?"

"I think I said he was easy to talk to."

"That, too. He went out drinking with the brother of one of Ron's friends last month. The kid supposedly committed suicide by slashing his wrists after washing down a bunch of pills in some alcohol. The brother doesn't believe the kid committed suicide."

And Beacher and Andrea had had their throats slit.

"The brother still had the kid's laptop computer so Beacher bought it from him. Want to guess what we found?"

Cassy realized she was holding her breath.

"Information on making bombs and rigging explosives."

"Gabriel, you have to tell someone!"

He didn't look away from the road. "The explosives used to kill your father came from a secured area on the base. Andrea didn't have access, but I did. So did Beacher. Someone had to give them those explosives."

Cassy was momentarily deflated. "I'm so confused."

"Welcome to my world."

There was no humor in his smile. The muscles in his neck were knotted. His hands gripped the steering wheel more tightly.

"But the computer—"

"Doesn't mean a thing since we had the opportunity to tamper with it. We learned that Ron and two of the others had been arrested at a military protest rally a year before the toxin was stolen. I think someone convinced them they could make a bigger statement by stealing the toxin."

"They'd kill millions of people to make a point?"

He shook his head. "That wouldn't have been their plan. Steal it, destroy the hard drives and research notes and get the public to help them demand stuff of that type be destroyed for good."

"But Dr. Pheng was probably using the toxin to work up an antidote!"

"I doubt the kids knew or cared. Idealists tend to have one-track minds."

"You think the kids killed my father?"

"If they did we'll never prove it now."

"There has to be *something!*"

His lips curved wryly. Chagrined, she realized her frustration was nothing compared with his.

"Beacher and I played 'pin the guilt' on every person we could think of and we kept coming back to Carstairs. The timing of his heart attack, the fact that he was away from the base during your dad's missing hours, that he had easy access to most places on the base and my presence when your father's house exploded all point to him, but it's all conjecture. We have no proof."

"There has to be a way to find some." Cassy fell silent trying to assimilate his words. "Is there any chance Beacher and Andrea actually were engaged?"

"No." The word was firm and uncompromising.

"Why would she tell the media they were?"

His jaw hardened. "As his fiancée, she'd gain information on the investigation into his death. She's always been impulsive."

"She's a lab tech!"

"I can't speak to her work ethics, but she'd get all

enthused about something for a while and then it would fizzle out."

Like their engagement?

"Marriage was her idea," he told her without inflection as if he'd heard her thoughts. "I doubt she'd have gone through with ours even if this hadn't happened."

"Then why...? Sorry. None of my business."

"She was attractive and the sex was great."

His voice was utterly flat, as if he were reporting the weather.

"It seemed like a good idea at the time."

There was nothing to say to that. "What are we going to do now?"

"Go shopping."

"But we have to see if Beacher found the toxin!"

"The opening tonight is semiformal."

Her lips parted in shock. "We're going to the gallery opening? We can't retrieve the package in front of a lot of people! Can we? Besides, if Rochelle thinks you're dead, won't she cancel the show?"

"Not a chance. Dead artists sell better than live ones."

"That's just wrong."

His lips curved slightly. "That's commerce."

"Shouldn't you at least call her?"

Gabe shook his head. "If I call Rochelle I draw attention to the exhibit. Sliffman and Huntington know I'm not dead. If they told her I'm alive, I'm sure she's been told to let them know if she hears from me. Whether they found the package or not, they'll be at the opening or have someone there in case I do show." He shot her a darkly amused glance. "Should be an interesting evening, don't you think?"

Cassy studied his expression. "I think you've watched too many James Bond movies."

He flicked on the radio with a grin.

"No radio?" Cassiopia asked dryly when nothing happened.

"Apparently not, but the roof keeps the rain off and the car runs."

"Small mercies. If Andrea was murdered because she knew something, why did someone try to kill you? They must have known you didn't have the vials or they wouldn't have blown up your house."

"Unless they didn't care."

"You think they *wanted* to release that toxin in that explosion?"

"That's one possibility. If they searched my house and didn't find it, they might have decided it was worth the risk as long as they were far enough away at the time to be safe."

That theory made a chilling sort of sense. "Everyone would believe you'd had it all along. The authorities would stop looking for anyone else."

"Not necessarily."

"But whoever's behind all this might think that!"

He shrugged. "I'm a loose end, Cassiopia. There's nothing anyone can use as leverage against me and I think someone feels they're running out of time. The authorities have never let up the pressure. Neither have Beacher and I. That stuff's out there somewhere. Sooner or later it's bound to surface and point fingers at the guilty party. If our thief has done his homework he knows I won't rest until I find out who killed Beacher."

He might be wounded, but this was one beast with

enough pride and fierce loyalty to drive him to complete whatever task he set for himself.

"I'm going to help you."

"I appreciate the offer, but it would be better if—"

"Don't say it! Like it or not, we're partners Gabriel. My dad is at least partly responsible for this situation. I will not allow thousands to die. Remember, someone wants me out of the way, too, so let's hit the mall."

THE LADY WAS A FORCE to be reckoned with. Gabe left her in the women's department and headed for the drug-store for a supply of ibuprofen. His cuts were throbbing and his headache had returned with aggravating intensity. Cassiopia's wrist probably hurt as well.

They were laden with packages and a suitcase apiece when they headed back to the small car. He dumped their parcels in the trunk and offered her the second bottle of cold water he'd purchased along with the ibuprofen.

"Mind reader."

He eyed her sling. "You all right?"

"I've been better. Now what?"

His cell phone rang before he could answer. Caller ID showed a number he wasn't familiar with. He had a feeling he knew who would be on the other end.

"Lowe," he answered.

"Len Sliffman. Don't hang up, Lieutenant."

Gabe waited in silence.

"You called in Andrea Fielding's murder."

Fast work. "Yes."

"Is Dr. Richards the woman who was with you? She's missing. We're concerned about her."

There was no point lying. "Yes."

"Do you know who killed Ms. Fielding?"

"No."

"We need to meet, Lieutenant."

"No."

"I don't believe you had anything to do with her murder. Or the explosion at your house," he added quickly.

"Who died?"

Cassiopia's anxious expression turned frightened. Sliffman hesitated.

"That's one of the things we need to talk about."

"No."

"All right, don't hang up! One of the men assigned to watch your place was a rookie. He saw someone enter through a dining room window and called for backup. When no lights went on he decided not to wait and went inside. He hit a trip wire on the stairs."

Exactly as Gabe had figured.

"Yours, or meant for you?" Sliffman asked.

"Not mine."

"We need to work together. Do you have the toxin?"

"No."

"Do you know where it is?"

"No."

Frustration filled Sliffman's voice. "Why would someone try to kill you?"

"When I find him, I'll ask."

Cassiopia worried her bottom lip. She gazed at him fretfully.

"Do you know why someone would kill Ms. Fielding?"

Gabe hesitated. "No, but you might take another look into the deaths of her brother and his friends."

This time the silence on Sliffman's end lasted several seconds.

"Talk to me, Lowe. What do you know?"

"Nothing I can prove."

"Believe it or not, I want to help."

"I've had enough government help."

Sliffman changed tactics. "Do you know why Ms. Fielding was getting ready to run?"

A hollow, sinking feeling filled his chest. Andrea had been dead long enough that rigor mortis had set in when he found her. He hadn't known she'd been about to rabbit.

"Her suitcases were in the trunk of her car," Sliffman continued. "She had an e-ticket for Tampa, Florida, in her purse. One way."

Sliffman had been Homeland Security's prime investigator when the toxin went missing and unlike the others Gabe had dealt with, Sliffman's questions had been direct and without malice.

Gabe knew all about good cop, bad cop, and he knew which role Sliffman had played and was still playing. But he also understood the job and respected it and the man. Still, Gabe wasn't prepared to put his welfare into the hands of anyone right now. The minute his freedom ended, so did his chances of solving this thing.

"I can't do much from a jail cell, Sliffman."

Cassiopia's eyes widened.

"What if I promise not to arrest you?"

"We both know you can't make that stick."

"If you aren't guilty, you won't go to jail."

"That's how it's supposed to work," Gabe agreed dryly. "Doesn't always."

Gabe closed his phone, dropped it to the pavement

and kicked it away as hard as he could. The phone sailed beneath a minivan. Cassiopia yanked on his arm.

"What are you doing?"

"Get in."

"Gabriel—"

He gave her no choice but to scramble around to the passenger side when he slid behind the wheel. She was still putting on her seat belt when he pulled out of the parking space. With any luck some poor fool would pick up the phone and use it, sending Sliffman's people on a wild-goose chase.

"It's possible to use global tracking to triangulate on a cell phone," he explained to Cassiopia. "Make sure yours is turned off. If it's emitting a signal it's a beacon to us. Sliffman got my number when I called 911. It will take him a little longer to get yours, but he'll get it, particularly now that he knows we're together. We can pick up new phones and pay for individual minutes if we need them."

Cassy fumbled in her purse and glared at him. "Why didn't you turn yours off, then?"

He pulled out of the parking lot. "I want to lead them to a dead end."

"Maybe you should have talked to him."

"I will when I have something to tell him."

"He didn't find the package?"

"I don't think so. He did tell me Andrea was leaving town."

"Why?" She closed her phone and put it back in her purse. "Why now? Why didn't she run when her brother was killed? Why would her killer wait all this time?"

"He appears to be cutting his losses all around."

"And we're on his list." Frustration laced her voice. "But we don't know anything!"

"He can't be sure of that. People with guilty consciences can make some wild assumptions. In this case I think he's making the same assumption we are, that Beacher found the toxin and gave it to me."

They were overlooking something and he knew it.

Chapter Nine

Gabriel was tired and he was hurting. Cassy saw it in the tight lines around his mouth and eyes. She wished the aspirin would kick in to stop the throbbing in her wrist. Trying on clothes had been difficult and she was tired.

She stopped talking, even when he drove into D.C. instead of Virginia. At least they were going against rush-hour traffic. He didn't offer an explanation and she decided not to ask until they pulled up in front of a costume store.

"You're kidding, right?"

A touch of humor lit his eyes. "You don't see me in a bunny suit?"

"You'd scare the heck out of all the other bunnies. A knight," Cassy corrected. "Dark, brooding, mysterious, but ready with your sword to smite the enemy."

Instantly, his expression closed down, becoming remote.

"Don't get fanciful. I'm no one's hero, Cassiopia."

"No? The armor's tarnished, but the image still fits." She reached for the door handle and stepped out into the light rain before he could reply.

Having never been inside a costume shop before she was fascinated, despite her aching wrist. While Gabriel walked over to speak with the older couple behind the counter, Cassy strolled between the rows of costumes. She paused near the back of the store at a display of wigs. A pretty, golden red one caught her eye. She was reaching out to touch the long strands when Gabriel came up behind her.

"I've always wanted to be a redhead," she said, grinning at him impishly.

"Try it on."

He didn't look as if he were teasing. "You're serious."

"I'm going for blond."

Cassy stood there with her mouth open as the owner began sorting through boxes of wigs underneath the display. She could hardly ask Gabriel what he was thinking with the older couple hovering nearby, especially when the wife walked over and offered to help Cassy try on the red wig.

Gabriel's flat look told her nothing. Bursting with curiosity, she allowed the woman to settle the long red strands on her head. In a nearby mirror, her gray eyes blinked back at her in surprise. The look wasn't bad, but it was different. In fact, it changed her entire appearance.

"We'll need to change your makeup, of course," the woman said seriously. "Hold on. I'll be right back."

"Looks good," Gabriel told her.

Astounded, she gaped at his own transformation. The man had helped him don a masculine, thick blond wig.

"You look like a surfer." She brushed back a strand of hair. "You can't be serious."

His lips curved. "I think it suits my playful side."

She very nearly asked what playful side but bit it back in time. She would have known Gabe's features anywhere no matter what color his hair was, but from the back, even from the side, it would take a second look and then recognition would be mostly because of the scar. The woman returned with a tray of makeup and handed her husband a jar of something.

"Now you just sit back and let me see what I can do," she suggested, pointing to some chairs at a counter off to one side.

Gabe was already taking a seat. Uncertainly, Cassy joined him at the small mirrored bar. He was going to let the man paint his face? This was too weird.

The woman was deft and sure as she worked on Cassy's face. "I used to be a makeup artist before Zeke and I retired and opened this place. Mostly theater in New York, but we worked more than a couple of movie sets, too. You've got good bones, honey, not like some of the people we've had to do. Good coloring, too. It makes it so much easier to change your look. You could have gone blond, you know. Most would, but not many can. I think you made a good choice with the red. The color suits you."

Cassy didn't know what to say. Fortunately, she didn't have to say anything. The woman chattered on about plays and the movie sets she'd worked on. At one time, she informed them, Zeke had been a costume designer. The two had met at the Kennedy Center some years ago where they'd both taken jobs.

"Your boyfriend says you want to fool some friends tonight. I think this should do it. What do you think?"

Cassy stared in the mirror at the transformation. While it wasn't a stranger who stared back, it wasn't her, either. She never wore eye makeup. In fact, she seldom wore more than lipstick and blush. The transformation was astounding.

"Wow."

The older woman beamed. "Always nice to know I haven't lost my touch."

Glancing at Gabriel she got another jolt. His scar was gone. A wiry blond beard, neatly trimmed, now hugged his jawline as if it had always been there. His eyebrows had been lightened and with the blond wig looking so natural, she'd take bets his own mother wouldn't have known him.

"I don't believe it."

He flashed her a genuine smile. "Zeke and Janet know what they're doing."

The older man looked pleased.

"I don't think anyone will recognize us tonight, what do you think?"

"I'm speechless."

The couple beamed, sharing smiles. Cassy watched Gabriel pay in cash, trying not to wince at the cost while she kept sneaking glances in the mirrors around the room to reconcile their new looks. Gabriel chatted easily with the couple about the surprise they were going to give their friends before they announced their engagement.

The last bit startled her so much she nearly gave them away by gasping out loud. A funny tingle in her midsection became electric when he slid his arm around her as naturally as if he did it all the time.

Cassy barely managed to go with the flow. It was all

she could do to pretend his easy conversation was something she was used to hearing when she'd never heard him talk so much. She couldn't help thinking this was probably the man he'd been before the toxin was stolen. It made her sad to think how badly that one incident had changed their lives.

Without thought, she leaned her head against his chest and let him talk them out of the shop when three new customers entered. The rainy day had given way to a dreary evening.

"What do you think?" he asked when they were in the car.

"Is that beard going to stay on?"

He grinned and her stomach fluttered. "The problem's going to come when I try to take it off. Itches like the devil."

"The beard?"

"And the wig."

Her own wig didn't itch exactly, but it was a strange feeling having something tight covering her scalp. She had to fold her hands to keep from touching it.

"How did you know about that place?"

"I dated a local actress once."

Of course he had. The old Gabriel must have been a ladies' man, like Beacher. He could be devilishly attractive. She'd thought so even when he was scaring the daylights out of her. And when he smiled one of those rare smiles, a woman didn't have a chance.

"Where are we going now?"

"You're going to rent a car," he told her.

"Why?"

"We're confusing our back trail."

"It's working. I'm confused."

Again the flash of humor that did disturbing things to her insides appeared.

"Why are we renting a car when we have this wonderful little wreck?"

"Because by now Sliffman knows about this car. Remember the two women in Andrea's parking lot?"

"Oh. Well, why didn't we rent a car in the first place?"

His lips twisted wryly. "Because I didn't think of it at the time. The used-car lot was right there. Can you drive with that arm?"

"If I take off the sling, but I'll need to use my driver's license. If they know I'm with you—"

"That won't matter. The people watching the gallery will be looking for this car. I plan to be in and out before they run this rental plate and make the connection." He hesitated. "You don't have to do this."

"No, but we both know I will."

Feeling strange in the wig and makeup, and minus her sling, Cassy walked to the rental place alone after he dropped her at the corner. He hadn't told her what sort of car to get so she rented a sporty, bright blue coupe and prayed she'd be able to drive it around the corner to the shopping center where he'd said he was going to park.

Part of her wondered if he'd be there or if this was a ploy to walk away from her. But she told herself he would have rented the car *before* taking her to the costume shop if that had been his intention.

Cassy tried not to use her left hand as she drove cautiously to the arranged spot and found him there, parked beneath an overgrown tree in the farthest, darkest corner of the lot. Despite the blond wig and makeup that covered his scar, Gabriel was still seeking out the shadowy places of the night. It made her heart ache for him.

She moved to the passenger's side while he transferred their packages to the backseat and small trunk of the rental.

"Did this thing come with sunglasses?" he asked.

Puzzled, she glanced at the light mist falling around them in the dark before she realized he was referring to the car's color.

"I like blue."

"So do I but this neon color stands out."

"Then you should have specified, or rented it yourself."

He scowled. "I don't match my driver's license picture at the moment."

"In case it's escaped your attention, neither do I, but they barely glanced at it."

"You're a woman," he pointed out, sliding behind the steering wheel.

"There's a typical masculine response."

"Here's your sling."

"Thanks." Cassy welcomed the material cradling her arm once more. Her body had begun complaining about this morning's tumble from the bike. Stiff and achy muscles accompanied her throbbing wrist.

"Now what?"

"Now we go back to the mall and use a restroom to change clothes for the reception."

"Why not check into a motel?"

"We want to stay a moving target. The minute we

settle we risk being found. Sliffman isn't going to roll over and wait for us to talk to him. He'll have people actively looking for us."

Cassy fell silent until they left the parking lot. "What time do we need to be at the gallery?"

"The reception's from seven to nine."

"We're going to be late. And won't we need an invitation to get in?"

"Technically, yes."

"Technically?"

There was irony in the curve of his lips. "We're going to fake it."

"This just keeps getting better."

"You could always wait outside," he offered.

CASSY HAD CHOSEN her outfit with care but there was no way to change without causing her wrist more pain, especially now that she didn't dare disturb her wig and makeup. The wide-legged black silk pants had an elastic waistband that pulled on easily, but required both hands. The full material looked like a skirt until she moved. She'd chosen it for the slash pockets deep enough to conceal a gun. A black satin, button-down blouse and matching jacket with a pair of satin heels rounded out the look. She wished she'd opted for flats instead, but the outfit required heels to complete the sophisticated look she was going for.

In the ladies' room mirror she barely recognized herself. The crystals Gabriel had given her were the perfect accent as they sparkled in the overhead lights. The black outfit set off her new red hair and the only thing that marred the look was her cloth sling. Cassy decided she could stuff it in the other pocket and hold her wrist against her waist. However, until they reached the gallery she'd keep the sling on for support.

She studied her reflection looking for an awkward bulge from the gun. Relieved when there wasn't one, she went to join Gabriel and found him waiting in the hall between the restrooms. Behind a pair of spectacles, his eyes gleamed in masculine approval the minute he saw her. Her heart beat a little faster when he strode forward to claim the bag of old clothing from her good hand.

"You look…perfect."

His voice sounded rusty. "Thank you. You look pretty good yourself."

While the dark sports coat, black turtleneck and slacks weren't a big departure from his normal attire, the outfit made a dramatic statement with his blond beard and hair. The look suited him.

"Where did you get the glasses?"

"At the drugstore when I picked up the ibuprofen."

"Nice touch. Can you see through them?"

"Well enough."

Cassy was aware they drew several eyes as he led her outside to the car. The force of his personality would command attention anywhere he went. Even if it was a farce, she felt good being escorted by him.

"We're running awfully late."

"Intentionally," he assured her. "We need to arrive at the height of things so we'll be less noticeable."

Women would always notice Gabriel, but she didn't tell him so.

"It won't take us long from here."

He had just enough time to rehearse her role for getting them inside and they were there.

GABE WAS FAIRLY CERTAIN the man checking invitations at the door would be one of Sliffman's people. He'd spotted a dark sedan with a view to the entrance and someone inside who was probably backup. Sliffman might or might not be here himself, but for certain, others would be.

They moved quickly to fall in behind another well-dressed older couple who appeared to be walking toward the door.

"Did you bring the invitation Gretchen gave us?" Cassy asked in a carrying voice.

"I thought you brought it."

"I told you I wasn't going to carry a purse tonight."

Gabe let annoyance show in his voice. "I didn't realize that meant you weren't going to bring the invitation."

"Since when was I put in charge? It probably doesn't matter anyhow. Surely Gretchen will have given them our name."

"Don't bet on it," he told her glumly.

"Oh, Perry, don't sulk. I know you didn't want to come in the first place, but what's the worst they can do? Send us away? If they do, we'll come back another time. If Gretchen hadn't said this sculptor was so good we wouldn't even be here. Tell you what, if they don't let us in we'll go over to that new place you've been wanting to try for dinner."

The older couple paused at the door to show their

invitation. The woman cast a sympathetic look Cassy's way while Gabe grumped about her blasted art collection.

"May I see your invitation?" the attendant asked in a bored voice.

Gabe scowled as he studied the man, looking for the telltale bulge that would show where he kept his gun. "My wife forgot it."

"I did no such thing, it was your fault. And it wasn't even our invitation. Gretchen Morrison offered us hers because she couldn't come tonight. Hopefully, she gave Rochelle Leeman our names. Perry and Bonnie Sturbridge?"

The man glanced at a clipboard. "I'm sorry, you're not on the list."

"I told you so," Gabe groused. "Now can we leave?"

The older couple had paused nearby. The woman, obviously listening, came back. "I'm certain you'll find Gretchen Morrison on your list," she told the man. "This couple is friends of hers."

He glanced down again and frowned. "I'll have to check on this."

"Do so. There's Rochelle now." She made an imperious motion to Rochelle, who hurried to obey the summons.

"Deborah, how good to see you! And Eric, so nice of you to come."

Gabe knew this was the moment when it could all fall apart but the flustered woman eyed Gabe and Cassy without a flicker of recognition.

"Is there a problem?"

"No invitation," the man told her, indicating them. "And their names aren't on the list."

Cassy stepped forward quickly.

"Ms. Leeman, I'm Bonnie Sturbridge. Gretchen Morrison is my godmother. She offered us her invitation but we left it at home. She told me I had to come and check out this new sculptor you're featuring. I don't remember his name."

"Gabriel Lowe. Yes, of course. It's all right, Ned. Please do come in. Gretchen was quite taken with Gabe's work. Are you a collector?"

"Newly started, I'm afraid. Perry just came into a generous inheritance and I'm trying to find some display pieces for our new house. Gretchen got me enthused and suggested we come tonight."

"Of course. I'm so glad you did. Come in and look around. If you'll excuse me for just a second…"

Rochelle turned to greet a man who'd entered behind them. The first couple had faded away and Gabe put his hand on the small of Cassy's back to steer her clear of the door.

"Nice," he whispered in her ear. She glowed up at him, eyes bright with relief and excitement.

"I was scared to death," she admitted, "but she didn't recognize you."

He turned down a glass of champagne from a passing waiter and Cassy did the same. "Don't get cocky."

"I'm too nervous for cocky. Look! That's one of your pieces over there, isn't it? And it's marked sold!"

Gabe felt a strange thrill as he stared at the sold sign on the Noah's Ark set he'd picked up only yesterday.

"I wonder how much she got for it?"

His eyebrows lifted in amusement even though he wondered the same thing. He couldn't believe it when they found a second piece also marked sold. This affirmed his talent in a way nothing else could have done.

The crouching lion held center stage in the second room and his heart lurched. *One* crouching lion.

"What's wrong?" Cassiopia whispered as he neared the sculpture and ran a hand along its flank.

"Where's the other one?" he muttered.

Her eyes widened. She cast around the room looking for the second lion, but he'd already seen that it wasn't there. Before she could say anything the couple they'd come in behind joined them.

"Amazing, isn't it?" the woman asked. "His work is so realistic. The artist was extremely talented."

"Was?" Cassiopia asked.

"You haven't heard? Oh, my dear, it's been all over the news. That house that blew up last night belonged to him."

Gabe listened even as he inspected the piece carefully.

"No way," Cassiopia exclaimed, putting just the right amount of shocked emphasis in her tone.

"I'm afraid so. Either he's the one who was killed or he's in very serious trouble. Rochelle doubled the asking price on his work as a result."

Gabe worked to control his reaction to that.

"You do know Gabriel Lowe is the man the FBI believed stole that deadly toxin five years ago. You must remember the case. The toxin was never recovered. I must say it makes one wonder."

It was on the tip of Gabe's tongue to ask her "Wonder what?" but she changed the subject with barely a pause for breath.

"Your husband seems very fond of this piece. Are you going to buy it?"

"Oh, no. It's too big for the space."

"Maybe," Gabe answered at the same time.

Cassiopia sent him a worried look. "Darling, where would we put it? We're just starting to collect. I wanted something more along the lines of the Noah's Ark pieces," she told the woman.

"Yes. Those *are* spectacular. I do hope more than one cast was made. I wouldn't mind owning that set myself. If there's only the one, the buyer's price will really jump with the artist being dead."

Cassy shuddered. Gabe moved quickly to her side. "We ought to think about the lion for the back garden," he told her.

"Surely you're jesting," the older woman said. "You don't put works like these outside."

"No?" He tapped the lion's head. "You think it would rust?"

Humor danced in Cassiopia's eyes. The woman made an excuse and hurried her husband away from them.

"That was mean," she told him.

"Yeah, well, we have to work our way over there. I need a look in the back room. Pretend an interest in that painting."

"Not that orange monstrosity!"

Gabe inclined his head. He pointed to the piece, urging her in its direction. "Rochelle's back room is beyond that door."

"I thought we were going to—"

"New plan. If anyone asks, I went in search of a bathroom."

Cassiopia bit at her lower lip as they made their way across the room, dodging waiters and guests alike. Gabe had been keeping his eyes peeled for Sliffman or Huntington, relieved not to see either of them. He didn't think his disguise would fool a professional like Sliffman up close.

Gabe halted them before the large blob of orange paint. The minute he saw an opening, he reached for the door handle beside it, and found it unlocked.

Slipping inside he turned on the light switch immediately. If he were caught, it would look more natural than if he pretended to be fumbling around in the dark. He didn't think he'd be long. Given the way things had been going so far, he had a sinking feeling he wasn't going to find the other lion.

He was right.

When he emerged he found Cassiopia chatting with an intense, birdlike woman in a scarlet dress who bobbed her head a lot and flung her arms about like a pair of broken wings. She was enthusing over the ugly painting. Gabe suspected she was the artist. Rochelle was heading in their direction and Gabe wasn't sure if she'd seen him come out of the room or not. While she hadn't recognized him yet, he wasn't about to press his luck.

"That wasn't the bathroom," he announced, interrupting the woman. "We have to leave."

"We just got here," Cassy protested on cue.

"Something I ate disagreed with me."

"Are you sure, Perry? I was just talking with—"

"Not now. I'm going to be sick. Sorry," he told the woman as Rochelle reached them.

"Are you enjoying the show?" she asked perkily.

"Very much," Cassiopia responded, "but I'm afraid my husband is ill. It's his own fault. I told him not to eat all that shrimp at lunch today, but would he listen? No. I told him it tasted a little off."

Gabe tried to look ill and groaned.

"Honestly, Perry," Cassiopia scolded. "This is so embarrassing. I'm sorry, Ms. Leeman, but the truth is, my stomach is a little upset as well. We're very interested in several pieces including this brilliant painting of Ms. Weissel's, but we're going to have to come back. Will you excuse us, please?"

"Of course."

With a perplexed frown, Rochelle stepped aside while Cassiopia continued to berate him as they hurried toward the entrance.

"Next time will you listen to me? If you throw up in front of all these people, Perry, I will never forgive you. Do you hear me? Never!"

"The whole block can hear you. I'm going to be sick and all you can do is complain."

They were past the alert attendant and out the door without being stopped, but Gabe didn't drop his role in case anyone was watching or listening.

"I think I may have ptomaine," he complained as he hurried them down the sidewalk. "Maybe I should go to the hospital." And in a barely audible whisper he added, "Keep going."

Cassiopia was so quick on the uptake he could

have hugged her. She stepped up the pace and continued her harangue.

"This is humiliating. I hate to think what Ms. Leeman will say to Gretchen when they talk. I hope you've learned your lesson. Next time, show some restraint at a buffet. You are such a pig when it comes to shrimp. This serves you right. I wasn't ready to leave and if someone buys that painting before I can get back here tomorrow, I'm going to be furious with you."

"I'm dying and all you can think of is some stupid painting?"

They reached the car and he handed her the keys. He knew her wrist was hurting. He'd seen the way she kept her arm pressed against her middle while she was listening to the artist, but it couldn't be helped.

Questions and fear were in her eyes, but Cassiopia said nothing as they pulled away from the curb. Gabe watched the mirrors. There was no sign anyone had followed them.

"Pull into that lot over there and we'll switch places," he told her. "We need to get back to the shopping center where we left the other car in case they run these plates."

"What about this car? And what about the lion and the package?"

"We'll leave this one on the rental lot and lock the key inside. The lion is gone."

She braked to a halt and stared at him wide-eyed. "What do you mean, gone?"

"That's the wrong lion on display."

Chapter Ten

"Are you sure?"

"Positive. Beacher and I built those bases. If you believe in the power of prayer, now would be a good time for one."

"Do you think the authorities have the other lion?"

Gabe scratched at his jaw where the spirit gum was irritating his skin. He felt drained and achy and scared at the same time. "No. I think Rochelle sold it."

"What are we going to do?"

"I don't know," he admitted. "Let me think about it."

Neither of them spoke as they drove to the parking lot where they'd left the car they'd purchased earlier. Gabe transferred their clothing and purchases back again.

"You're going to have to return this rental to the lot," he told her. "Park it in front of the door, put the key under the mat, lock it and walk to the corner. I'll wait there for you. It probably won't matter, but if the lot has surveillance cameras I'd rather not have our license plate show up on them."

She looked as drained as he felt, but nodded gamely.

When she joined him a few minutes later it was obvious they had both run out of steam. She didn't even ask where they were going.

Gabe headed north, keeping to the city streets. As soon as they crossed into Maryland he started looking for motels. When he spotted a likely candidate he pulled into a nearby chain restaurant.

"I'm not hungry," she protested.

"Neither am I. Wait here. I'll be out in a few minutes."

HE WAS GONE MORE THAN a few minutes. Cassy was about to go in and check on him when he came striding out, a bag of food tucked under one arm. The beard and wig were gone and he was carrying his jacket. He'd put his glasses back in place, mussed his hair and retained the putty that covered his scar. Once again his look was altered just enough that anyone who didn't know him well would have had to look twice to recognize him.

She hadn't been hungry, but now the scent of roast turkey woke her sleeping appetite.

"I needed an excuse to use their restroom so I hope you like turkey and coconut cream pie. I'll get us checked in over there and we can eat in the room."

She took the bag and tried not to salivate as the smells reminded her that lunch had been hours ago. The room proved to be remarkably similar to the one the night before. Different colored paint, paper and bedspread, but the layout was much the same.

While Gabe went to the drink machine in the hall, Cassy laid out their meals.

"Not exactly gourmet fare," he told her around a bite of turkey.

"Good, though. I was hungry after all. Your face is red, you know."

"The spirit gum irritated the skin."

Gabe turned on the television set and they ate in silence. An inane sitcom kept them from thinking too much. Halfway through her slice of pie, Cassy put her plastic fork down.

"What are we going to do?"

Gabriel took a long swallow of his bottled water before answering.

"When Rochelle introduced me to Gretchen Morrison she said Mrs. Morrison was a very important customer."

"Uh-huh. That's why we used her name."

"Right. The lions weren't crated. They must have gone on the truck last. I'm guessing Rochelle showed them to Mrs. Morrison and she bought one then and there."

"But wouldn't Rochelle have waited to let her take it until after the show? You said she wanted them for the centerpiece."

"I doubt she'd argue with a good customer, especially since she was never supposed to have had both lions in the first place."

"Then we'll have to go see Mrs. Morrison."

His surprised expression would have been comical another time. "I'll go see Mrs. Morrison. You get some rest."

"I don't think so. It will seem less threatening if we both go to see her."

"I wasn't planning to visit her exactly."

"You're going to break into her house?" Of course he was.

"Don't worry about it."

"I'll worry if I want. I'm going with you."

"No, you aren't. I can do this better alone."

"No doubt." She grinned up at him, remembering her inept attempt to enter his house. "But I'm going anyhow." She held up a hand to stave off his next protest. "I'm a quick study. I won't get in the way. Do you really think I could sleep while you go over there alone?"

"No."

He stood, his features hard and uncompromising.

Cassy glared right back. "You walk out that door and I'm calling Sliffman."

"You won't."

"Wrong." She put all the conviction she could into her voice and her glare. "I've done nothing they can arrest me for and if you aren't going to protect me, he will."

She saw at once that she'd fully roused the beast and he was most intimidating. Still, she refused to flinch or back away despite every instinct that urged her to sit down and make herself as small as possible.

"Tonight, I proved I can be an asset," she told him, proud that her voice didn't quaver.

"Yes, but this time I'm breaking in to a house, not a party. And that *is* a criminal act."

"I can live with it if you can. I've already broken in to your house. Twice."

She shouldn't have reminded him. He didn't need ammunition for why she shouldn't go with him.

"But this time you'll go to jail if we're caught."

"Then make sure we don't get caught."

For a minute she thought she'd pushed him too far. Gabriel could have posed for one of his crouching lion sculptures. Every muscle and sinew was tensed to strike.

"If you were a man I'd deck you."

"If I were a man we wouldn't be having this conversation." She wasn't sure where the courage to face him down was coming from but she could not afford to relent. "You'd take Beacher along, wouldn't you?"

"You aren't Beacher."

"No, but I'm the best you have. While you look up her address, I'll put my jeans back on."

She started to push past him. He grabbed her shoulders firmly enough to hold her in place, but not hard enough to bruise.

"Why?"

She reminded herself that he was a wounded beast with no reason to trust. But he needed someone to trust and she wanted that someone to be her.

"Because I'm scared and I'm tired and I want this over. And we both know it won't be over until we know what Beacher found."

"It may not be over even then."

"But we'll have tried. *I'll* have tried."

"Because of your father?"

She hadn't given any thought to her father, but said, "That, too."

His eyes bore into hers. She held that gaze. There was only an instant to recognize the change in his expression before he lowered his face, drew her body against his and claimed her mouth.

Once again it was not a gentle kiss, but Cassy didn't want gentle from him. The fluttery feeling in her stomach became a warmth that quickly blazed. She used her good hand to pull him even closer and kissed him back. Her legs turned to jelly while her insides melted. She felt the press of his erection against her leg and was elated. She wanted him just as much.

GABE PULLED BACK, struggling for a control that should have come easily. It was anything but. Touching her had been a serious mistake. He wanted her with a hunger that blunted common sense. And she wanted him, too, scars and all. That knowledge was heady.

The bed was right there. A simple nudge and she'd be flat on her back, as open, needy and willing as him to sate this driving urge.

"You're playing with fire," he growled.

She shook her head. Her silky hair tumbled about her shoulders. "A lion."

"Lions maul their mates," he warned. "I don't want you getting hurt, Cassiopia."

"That's not high on my list, either, but I make my own decisions."

He was pretty sure they were having a conversation on two levels at once. The words applied to tonight's planned activity as well the one they were close to having in the large bed that beckoned them.

He kissed her again. She made a slight mew of protest and he gentled the kiss, all desire to punish her gone. This kiss asked, rather than demanded, and she responded instantly.

Gabe thought he might never get enough of the taste and feel of her body against his. He groaned, low in his throat, and forced his hands to set her aside. Humming with unfulfilled desire he found he was shaking. Shaking!

She took an unsteady step back. Her mouth had a bruised, just-kissed look, her gaze sexily slumberous.

"I'll be right out."

Her voice wasn't close to steady.

"Wait for me."

Gabe groaned and turned away. She made her way into the bathroom, trusting him to do as she demanded. Torn, he stood there. She came back out to reach for the bag of clothes they'd purchased earlier.

He could still leave, but he knew he wouldn't. She amused him, angered him, tantalized him and in general drove him crazy, but he wanted her like no one else, ever. And he wouldn't be able to forgive himself if anything happened to her.

Only a fool would let her come along tonight but if he hadn't been a fool he never would have touched her in the first place. So much for military discipline. His emotions were a tangled mess.

Her father's death would always be there between them. She might want him physically, but once her passion ebbed and she started thinking again she'd be appalled. As long as Gabe remembered nothing of what happened that day, even finding the toxin wouldn't prove his innocence.

Why hadn't Beacher told Gabe what he was doing? Why had he gone off on his own to play hero?

Wasn't that exactly what Cassiopia accused Gabe of trying to do?

This time his groan of frustration came for an entirely different reason. He reached for the phone book tucked beneath the nightstand and wished he could get the taste and feel of Cassiopia out of his head.

THERE WAS NOTHING like a little sexual tension to make a woman forget all her other aches and pains, Cassy decided. She managed the stretch jeans with their elastic waistband, but thought better of the white blouse. If they were going to break into a house she needed to wear dark colors, so she left her fancy blouse on.

She was about to commit a felony. Again. Yet all she kept thinking about was what would happen here in this motel room *after* they got back.

Assuming they didn't get caught.

Gabe was waiting when she entered the room and reached for the jacket.

"You do what I say, when I tell you or you stay here. Clear?"

Cassy gave him a curt nod, afraid to trust her mouth with words. This was no time to argue. Gabriel didn't look satisfied, but he led her back out in the rain to the car without a word.

Gretchen Morrison's house was huge and tucked away among the trees on top of a hill. The only way to get there was up a steep, narrow driveway. Gabriel made a U-turn and parked on the exposed side of the road down below.

"This car will stand out in this neighborhood," she warned.

"I know, but it's not like we can leave it at the end of the block."

No, the block was close to a mile long in the direction they'd come from and who knew how far down it continued. Each estate had acreage and all of it wooded.

"The car would have never made this hill," she huffed as they trudged up the incline. "I'm not sure I will. I'd hate to live here in winter."

There was a flash of teeth, as he must have smiled.

Moisture dripped from the canopy of trees overhead. The rain had stopped again, but thanks to the trees they were thoroughly wet by the time they reached the house, where fear stopped her in her tracks. Gabriel also halted as they stared at the black Jaguar parked in the turnaround out front. Few windows faced this side of the house and most of those were on the second level. All were ablaze with light.

"That's not good."

"No," Gabriel agreed. "Wait here while I check the sides and back. Call out if anyone comes up the drive."

Privately, Cassy was relieved. She had no desire to get any closer to this solemnly intimidating structure.

Gabriel vanished, becoming one with the shadows. He was entirely too good at doing that. The military should have put him in covert operations. He was a natural.

Cassy studied the parked car in the weak glow from the porch light. A dented scrape along the front fender marred the car's pristine finish. She was about to move closer for a look at the license plate when the front door swung open.

Cassy pressed against the nearest tree. A figure hurried outside and ran straight to the waiting Jag without giving her a glimpse of his face despite the additional light spilling from the front door. The dome light didn't go on as he climbed inside and started the engine.

Frozen in place, Cassy held her breath. Headlights swept past within inches of where she stood. The car didn't slow. It rolled down the steep drive with more speed than sense.

Gabriel emerged out of nothing beside her. The scream of his name choked in her throat unuttered.

"I saw. Did you get a look at him?"

She shook her head.

"Come on."

Quaking, she followed. They were at the front door before her stunned brain kicked in. Surely he didn't intend to go in there? Couldn't he see something was wrong?

He nudged the door open with his foot. It bounced back against something on the floor out of sight. Gabe swore beneath his breath.

"Wait."

Cassy had already stopped moving and was racked with uncontrollable shaking now. She glimpsed a pale thin arm stretched out against the cold, hard slate floor and her stomach rebelled. The last time she'd entered an unlocked door, she'd found Beacher's body.

REGRET HIT HIM as Gabe took in the scene, and summoned a professional detachment. Gretchen Morrison had supported her last artist. Her frail body was sprawled in a pool of her own blood. The coppery smell of death clung to the air. Her throat had been slit so deeply that the cut had nearly severed her head.

From the position of the body and the blood splatters, Gabe was fairly certain she'd opened the door to her attacker. She'd either turned her back to him or he'd forced her around to strike the killing blow. It wouldn't have taken much force. She had been a fairly small woman.

But her killer had been sloppy. He'd stepped in her blood on his way down the hall. Several clear, running footprints led away from the scene. He must not have noticed them against the dark stone floor.

Going inside would compromise the crime scene, but

Gabe had no choice when he spotted the crouching lion in the foyer to his right. His sculpture had obviously been positioned to stand guard at the bottom of the open stairway that led to the second floor. Someone had pushed the piece over on its side.

Gabe removed his wet shoes and stepped inside, quickly moving to the lion. He was careful not to step where the killer had. There were blood smears on the cold metal, but the hidden compartment was still closed, giving him hope.

Gabe opened the hidden panel at the back of the base with trepidation. He fully expected to find the package gone, but it was still nestled inside. He scooped it out, wiped where he had touched, closed the panel and stood.

His heart landed in his throat as his gaze traveled down the opposite hall to a wheelchair sitting there. No wonder the killer had gone to his left first. Gretchen Morrison hadn't died alone.

Gabe didn't have to cross to the victim to see that the man slumped there had tried to flee. He must have called out to Gretchen and summoned death instead.

Sickened, Gabe returned to the front door and handed Cassiopia the package before he stepped outside and put his shoes back on. She gazed at him with eyes that were too wide and filled with horror. He was thankful she hadn't seen what he had.

He took her arm and hurried her back down the steep driveway. Not until they reached the car and began driving away did she speak.

"I didn't get his license plate number," she whispered.

He glanced at her, worried she might fall apart, but her bleak gaze was steady. She'd hold it together.

"I did."

"We need to report this."

"We will."

"I'm going to be sick."

"No, you won't."

She shut her eyes and leaned her head back, swallowing hard. She was trembling. He felt shaky himself. There might have been other people inside that house. He should have checked, but it was too late now. Bitterly, he drove well away from the area before he started looking for a public telephone. They weren't as plentiful as they used to be now that everyone carried a cell phone, but a brightly lit gas station on a busy corner had one and he pulled over.

Cassiopia said nothing when he got out and made the call. Minutes later they were back on the road. Her eyes were shut, but Gabe knew she wasn't sleeping. He pulled into a beer-and-wine shop. She merely nodded without opening her eyes when he told her he'd only be a minute and went inside.

Her silence worried him, but he didn't feel much like talking, either. As soon as they arrived back at the motel she handed him the package and went into the bathroom and closed the door.

Gabe listened for the sound of retching that never came. After a few minutes he heard water running and relaxed. He poured her a glass of white wine and opened a bottle of beer. The alcohol wouldn't help rid him of the taste of death, but he needed it all the same.

THE WATER HELPED SOME, but Cassy still felt ill as she left the bathroom to face Gabriel. He was waiting in one of the chairs, an open bottle of beer in his hand. The wrapped package sat on the table beside him. He'd opened a bottle of wine as well and poured her a glass.

Such a small thing, it shouldn't make her want to cry. She moved forward, lifted the glass and drank it straight down. The wine churned in her stomach.

"You'll get sick," he cautioned.

"Probably. Are you going to open that?" The package was the right size for a thick, oversized paperback book.

"I thought I'd let you do it."

She poured another glass of wine but didn't drink it. "This isn't a lab."

"Do you need one?"

For an answer, she reached for the package. Her hands were surprisingly steady. The toxin needed liquid as a catalyst. They should be safe. Nevertheless, she unwrapped the box with care.

A white envelope with *Gabe* scrawled across the face had been taped to the outside of a black box. Cassy removed the note gently and handed it to him without a word.

Gabriel stared at his name for a second. The pulse in his temple throbbed. He turned the envelope over and opened it with care. There was a single sheet of paper inside.

"Buddy," he began to read aloud, *"if you're reading this I'm in big trouble or dead."*

Cassy swallowed hard, forcing the image of death aside.

"Dr. Richards outsmarted the bastards, but his daughter pointed me in the right direction."

She caught her breath.

"I left the toxin where I found it, but here's the documentation. The hard drive is encrypted but the notes aren't. I'm leaving this with you because I think Andrea followed me to Sunburst. If so, she knows I found something. I need to go talk to her."

Gabriel's jaw clenched. The vein in his forehead throbbed with life.

"If something happens to me, dig at her. Dr. Pheng might know if she was involved with Carstairs or anyone on base besides you, but here's something interesting. I learned Huntington's wife is spending big all of a sudden. Where's all that money coming from on a major's salary?"

Cassy heard growing anger in Gabe's voice.

"The word is that Huntington's going to be passed over for promotion and plans to retire. We both know he has no love for you so be careful. I spotted a black Jag following me twice now."

Cassy inhaled sharply.

"Find out who owns one or has access to one. I'm sure you're pissed at me right now, especially if I got myself killed, but things fell into place fast after I talked with the daughter. I had a hunch and it paid off. You couldn't have come with me into Sunburst so I didn't bother to tell you about it and I'm not going to tell you what I'm doing now, either, because you'd insist on coming with me, and Andrea won't talk if you're there. She knows something. I know she does. I'll explain everything tonight. You know how much I always wanted to be a hero, but if I don't make it back to pick this up…"

Gabriel's voice suddenly faltered.

"...it's my own damn fault, not yours. Don't get yourself killed trying to avenge my stupidity. Go out and live your life, Gabe. Do it for me, buddy. You're the brother I always wanted. I hereby make you personally responsible for the contents of my not-so-little black book. There's bound to be someone in there that can put up with a loner like you. Love ya, pal. Beacher."

GABE COULDN'T SWALLOW past the tight constriction in his throat. The hollow pain of loss was so acute his vision blurred. He stood abruptly, dropping the note to the table. He didn't look at Cassiopia as he walked out the door. He needed space. He needed to move. He wanted to hit something or someone. He wanted Beacher alive, that friendly, boyish face beaming at him as Gabe trounced him at handball or sat with him over a beer.

CASSY WATCHED HIM GO, tears threading their way down her cheeks. She didn't call out or try to stop him. He needed to grieve in private and she understood. She sat in the chair and cried for the dead and for Gabriel. When she finished, she splashed water on her blotchy face and organized their earlier purchases, changing into the sweatpants and shirt she'd bought to sleep in.

The box sat where they'd left it. She tossed the wrapping paper in the wastebasket and neatened the room. When there was nothing left to do, she pulled off the sweatsuit and climbed into bed naked.

She was wide-awake and waiting when Gabriel returned, his cold, remote mask solidly in place. He smelled of sweat and despair. She guessed he'd been running. As a stress reliever, she approved, but her heart ached for him. He was so alone.

He said nothing as he took clothing from his bag and went into the bathroom. Cassy settled when she heard the shower start up. The worst was over. He was grieving in his own way, but at least he wasn't bottling it up completely. She was pretty sure he'd been crying.

Even though she'd pulled back the covers on his side of the bed, Gabe didn't use them. He came out in yet another turtleneck pullover and pair of jeans, turned off the single light she'd left on for him and laid flat on his back on top of the blankets.

His voice came out of the dark, husky, with a tight edge. "As of now, you're out of it."

She rolled to face him, though she couldn't see his features in the dark room.

"You want me to end up like the others? I'm safer with you."

"I can't protect you, Cassiopia."

There was such pain in him. She touched his face and his body went stiff.

"You're the only one who can," she told him softly.

"Don't." He drew her hand away.

"I need to touch you. I need to feel alive. I need *you*."

"No!"

She gripped his hand, feeling the puckered skin of his burns. She lifted it to her mouth and kissed it tenderly.

"No."

But he didn't pull free.

"Fate made us partners, Gabriel. I'm going to make us lovers."

Chapter Eleven

Gabe knew he should roll away from the temptation of her, but God help him, he didn't want to. He craved her touch like a starving man. Beacher's note had ripped him to shreds and the run had left him exhausted. And while his grief seemed overwhelming, her touch brought him to life in a way he hadn't felt in years.

No woman had ever made love to him before. He'd always taken the lead. And as her lips and hands moved over him, it took massive control not to reach for her. When she touched his burnt skin with tender, almost reverent lips, Gabe tried to pull back. He'd actually forgotten about his many scars for a moment.

"No," she demanded. "Let me. They're the scars of a hero, not something to be ashamed of."

"I'm no one's hero," he growled. Beacher had wanted to be a hero and now he was dead.

"Mine," she whispered.

The word had the sound of a vow. He trembled inside but there were too many conflicting emotions to sort. Too much to feel, to taste, to hunger for.

"Stop, Cassiopia." But he didn't want her to stop. Not

ever. He held her away with unsteady hands. "These aren't the only scars." He couldn't bear her knowing how much damage had been done. Even without the light on she would know what his clothing hid if she continued.

"Let me see."

"No." He pulled away and rolled to his side.

"Do you really think I'm that shallow, Gabriel? Do you think the sight of a few scars will send *me* running?"

No, she wouldn't run. She would stay and her pity would be worse. Much worse.

"There's more than a few scars," he told her gruffly. "A section of burning siding landed on me while I was unconscious. I'm not a pretty sight."

"I'm sorry for what you went through, Gabriel. I can't even imagine how awful it must have been, but physical beauty isn't the measure of a person."

He shifted uncomfortably. She didn't understand. She couldn't possibly. "Look, just forget the whole thing and get some sleep. We have to be out of here first thing in the morning."

She sat up. Before he could stop her she'd turned on her bedside light. The blanket and sheet pooled at her waist revealing both silken breasts, the nipples hard and pointed.

"No. We need to talk about this."

Gabe groaned.

"I want you and you want me, too."

He didn't want to be having this conversation and he wished she'd pull up the blanket and cover herself.

"Don't push me aside, Gabriel. I'm not Andrea."

"Andrea has nothing to do with this!" Frustrated and angry, he glared at her.

She didn't even flinch at the lash of his words.

"Of course she does. She rejected you when you needed her the most, but it's been almost four years. Time to move on, Gabriel. You have to lower those formidable barriers you put up to keep everyone at a distance. It's time to let go and take a chance. With me."

Bitterness twisted his insides. "What gives you the right to judge me? You want to see scars, lady?" He reached for the hem of his shirt. "I'll show you scars."

"No! Not like this!"

She yanked on his hands before he could get the shirt up and over his head. They struggled briefly before she winced and drew back. The sight of her tears wrenched something loose inside him.

"I don't want to cause you more pain. I never wanted to do that." Her voice was thick with the tears starting to trickle down her cheeks. "I know I'm outspoken and pushy and I usually say the wrong thing, but this is about me, too. This is about how you feel about me! Whether you admit it or not, you're comparing me to the woman who walked away from your pain while you were in a hospital bed. But if you're going to keep judging every woman by her standards then I hope you enjoy living the life of a hermit."

With a sob, she started to leave the bed. He reached for her, pulling her back down, careful this time not to hurt her when she struggled briefly. She wouldn't look at him as she began to cry in earnest. His own cheeks were damp, but he couldn't stand her pain.

"I'm sorry. I'm sorry."

Because she was right. He *was* afraid to take a

chance. He was afraid she'd be so repulsed that she'd leave, but if he didn't try he'd lose her and he didn't want to lose her.

Gabe held her against his chest, resting his head on her silky hair, barely feeling the tears that soaked his shirt and streaked his face.

She was right. He was afraid.

There's bound to be someone that can put up with a loner like you, Beacher had written. Even Denny had tried to force him from his self-imposed isolation. Did he really want to live the rest of his life alone?

He and Cassiopia couldn't have forever. Unless his memory miraculously returned she could never be entirely sure what role he'd played in her father's death and neither could he, but it didn't matter. Not right now. Not tonight.

She pulled back, rubbing at her eyes furiously. Her face was puffy and blotchy. Hair tangled about her face. Tenderly, he regarded her, lifting her chin with his knuckle.

"Can we start over?"

"Why?"

"Because I need you to teach me how to trust again."

He dropped his hand when she said nothing. He'd blown it, and he'd lost something important. Something he hadn't even known he'd been missing.

"Take off your shirt."

Her voice was low, still clotted by the aftermath of tears. His gaze slid to the light and back to her face. She waited impassively. He could do this. He had to do this. For both of them.

Without rushing, he eased the shirt over his head.

He'd thought he'd been prepared for any reaction. But she examined him in silence, giving him no idea what she was thinking. And when she leaned toward him and placed her lips gently against a puckered ridge of skin, his eyes welled with fresh moisture.

"That wasn't so bad now, was it?"

He didn't know how to express the rush of emotions he was feeling. "What are you doing to me?"

"Loving you."

Gabe pulled her to him, saying with his lips and tongue what he couldn't with words.

He had to help her with his snap and zipper. Mindful of her wrist, he shucked pants that had become too tight, still uncomfortable as he bared even more scars on his hip and leg. Cassiopia insisted on kissing each one.

He couldn't put names to all his emotions, but she was going too slow with her tasting and touching. Barely trying, she was leading him ever closer to the brink. He wanted her now. And when she took him in her mouth, he nearly lost all control.

"My turn," he demanded gruffly, setting her aside.

Her smile of feminine satisfaction edged him another step closer. He paid homage to her mouth and throat and breasts, before working his way down her belly until her sweet cries became demands matching his own.

Gabe rolled on his back, pulling her with him, struggling to allow her to set the pace. She mounted him with exquisite slowness. Exerting every ounce of control he had left, Gabe let her settle, slick and tight and abruptly, as eager as he to release the incredible tension.

He swallowed her soft cry as she clenched around him. Control vanished in driving need and exquisite release.

For a very long time they lay together while their bodies cooled and their heartbeats mingled. Gabe thought he might be willing to hold her like this for the rest of his life. But after a while the back of his head and his leg began to throb. Cassiopia rolled off to one side, wincing as her bandaged wrist hit the mattress.

"Are you all right?"

She gazed at him and her smile lit his soul. "Never better."

And she curled against him trustingly and closed her eyes. After a few minutes, he closed his as well. He should get up and turn off the light, but it seemed like entirely too much effort.

He awoke to find the light still on and her pressed against him spoonstyle. His hand rested on the flatness of her belly while his arousal pressed against the rounded cheek of her butt. Gabe couldn't resist the impulse to slide his hand over the globe of her breast. Instantly, the nipple budded beneath his palm, rigid, tempting him to rub and pinch it to hardness.

Her breathing changed the moment he touched her. She made a soft sound of acceptance and pressed back against him, moving in invitation. Gabe swept aside the spill of her hair to reveal the long, smooth length of her neck. He kissed her there while pulling her more tightly against him until he could slide inside her. She sighed in welcome as she tightened around him.

In the soft gray light of early morning, augmented by the softly glowing bedside lamp, they made love slowly, learning each other's bodies with gentle eagerness until they were damp and too spent to move.

"GOOD MORNING TO YOU, TOO," Cassy told him some time later. "We left the light on all night."

"I noticed."

She didn't want to move, but she was stiff and sore all over and her wrist was throbbing painfully.

"Did I hurt you?" he asked.

"Do I look hurt?"

"You winced."

"Because my bladder is going to explode and I'm too comfortable to move."

"Yes."

She couldn't help grinning. "Don't revert. Complete sentences, remember?"

His eyes twinkled. "Too much effort."

And she was just thinking how much younger and relaxed he looked when his eyes began to cloud. Their idyllic moment was over. He rolled off the bed in a fluid motion.

"Do you want the bathroom first?"

"You're up. You can go ahead."

He entered the room without another word.

Now she did wince. Gabriel was an intensely private person. She suspected he hadn't always been that way. Given the extent of his injuries it was surprising he was even alive. She'd pushed him to reveal something painfully private last night while he was still grieving over the death of his best friend. She needed to be patient now. He needed time to accept all that had happened. Her wounded beast had begun to heal, but the process wouldn't happen overnight.

When Gabe came out a few minutes later she scooted past as he reached for last night's discarded jeans.

"I'll load the car while you take your shower," he called after her. "We can grab something to eat on the way."

"Deal," she agreed, wondering *on the way* to where?

Why did the morning after have to feel so awkward? Nobody needed all these stupid insecurities. Was he sorry? Could they both accept the night for what it was? Great sex.

Okay, stupendous sex. But sex. Not a lifetime of commitment. It wasn't as if she had never gone to bed with a man before. However things shook out, she was not going to regret what had passed between them last night. Or this morning. She smiled at the memory. She would take things one day at a time and try not to worry.

Or think the situation to death.

He had a steaming cup of coffee waiting when she came out.

"You are a god," she told him gratefully. And she would swear his neck reddened. He stepped quickly inside the bathroom and shut the door without replying. It would take time to teach him how to relax and have fun again.

And it wouldn't happen while they were in hiding for their lives.

Ignoring the television, she lifted the box that sat on the desk. After a moment's indecision, she opened it. One of the small notebooks her father had favored whenever he was working on a new project sat on top of the hard drive. Her father always claimed he thought better when he could scribble notes out in longhand before transferring them to the computer.

Love for him mingled with the sadness of her loss. She remembered all the times she'd seen her dad poring over notebooks like this one in his office at home and she suddenly missed him so much. She had a feeling he would have approved of Gabe.

Her coffee sat forgotten as she idly began scanning his notes in their neat, precise small script. While his field wasn't her area of expertise, she understood the basics. Apparently, her father had been doing a peer review of Dr. Pheng's work.

She began flipping through the pages. Her dad tended to write personal asides in his private journals as he thought an idea through. These notes weren't meant for others, they were a way of organizing his thoughts, but words like *ridiculous* and *preposterous* jumped out at her.

This was so typical of him, and yet the more she read, the more puzzled she became. Sequences had been underlined. Her dad's impatience and annoyance came through as clearly as though he were speaking.

Taking up the small pad of paper the hotel provided, she began making her own notes. She wasn't a chemist, but even she could see why her dad had been puzzled. "You're right, Dad, why would this have that result?"

"What result?"

Startled, Cassy looked up to find Gabriel standing there with his neatly combed hair still damp. He was dressed in yet another dark turtleneck shirt, pants and a sweatshirt that didn't hide the breadth of his shoulders or the trimness of his waist and hips. He was every inch an alpha male and his scars only enhanced the effect.

She sucked in a breath and let it out again at the flash of renewed desire. His eyes darkened as if he sensed her thoughts.

Arrogant male. He probably had.

"Dad was doing a peer review of Dr. Pheng's work.

That's not surprising given they're the leading experts in their field. From these notes I'd say they were working on possible antidotes to the toxin in the event it was ever used." She tapped the notebook lightly with her nail.

"I don't have a security clearance so I shouldn't even be looking at this."

She began putting things away. "I need to burn the few notes I did make so I don't get in real trouble. You wouldn't happen to have a match or a lighter, would you?"

"No. And this isn't the place." He nodded to the overhead sprinkler system.

"Good point."

"We'll burn them outside."

"Only if you find a match."

"Wait here."

Alpha male indeed. She really was going to have to work on his communication skills.

Her stiff muscles had loosened in the shower, but they were beginning to make themselves felt once again. Her wrist throbbed and she was aware of a multitude of bruises and new aches.

"Where should we put this box with the hard drive?" she asked as soon as Gabriel came back through the door.

He nodded toward his suitcase. "Unless you want to hold on to it."

Cassy had purchased a large shoulder bag when they'd gone shopping. She thought it might fit inside and it did.

"I thought of a way we can get rid of this hard drive that won't lead back to us," she told him. "What if we buy a shipping box and stick it in the mail? We can address it to Homeland Security and let them deal with it. We could even enclose a note telling them where to look for the vials. The authorities might suspect you were responsible but if we don't leave any prints they won't be able to prove anything."

Gabriel didn't look enthusiastic. "It has merit."

"But?"

"The minute we turn that hard drive over to anyone we lose the only edge we have. Are you all set?"

"Yes, but I don't understand. Aren't we in danger? Holding on to this seems like a really bad idea."

He nodded, but waited until they were outside to explain further. "If the killer suspects the toxin is out of reach, he's going to disappear. Right now he's desperate, making sloppy mistakes."

"He seems pretty efficient to me."

"You're still alive," he reminded her, "and you saw him."

"I never saw his face."

Gabriel opened the car door. Sandwiched between the car door and a privacy fence at his back, he pulled out a book of matches with the hotel's logo imprinted.

"Give me the notes you made."

Cassy peered around nervously before handing them over. Gabriel produced a small tin ashtray he'd appropriated from somewhere and burned them one sheet at a time. He even burned the rest of the hotel pad that was still blank. And as each page finished, he dumped the ashes in a small mud puddle and ground them beneath his foot.

"That was effective."

Gabe offered her one of his rare smiles. Cassy walked to the passenger's side feeling inexplicably good. As soon as they were moving she resumed their conversation.

"What sort of mistakes is the killer making, Gabe?"

"He killed the wrong person at my house."

"But he doesn't know that, does he?"

"Unless Huntington is our killer. Otherwise, if Sliffman's as good as I think he is I suspect he'll ask the media to downplay their coverage temporarily. Gretchen Morrison's murder will work to our advantage by giving the media a new focus. That's where the killer made his biggest mistake to date. He left evidence at the crime scene."

"What evidence?"

"Footprints in the blood."

Cassy swallowed hard.

"He set the bloody knife on top of the crouching lion and probably left more evidence throughout the house. I didn't go any farther than the foyer because once I realized he hadn't found the hidden compartment I took the package and left. I suspect he missed it because he was rattled by the presence of the man in the wheelchair."

"What man in a wheelchair?"

"Mrs. Morrison wasn't alone in the house. There was an older man in a wheelchair."

Thankfully, he didn't say more. Cassy didn't need details. Her stomach wanted to revolt. The image of Beacher was still fresh in her mind.

"We have to stop him."

"We will." Flat and uncompromising.

"How did he know to go after the lion?"

"He's trying to tie off loose ends. He knows or suspects Beacher recovered something and passed it to me. He turned over the lion to be sure the base was solid and nothing was hidden inside. Only a few of my pieces are large enough and have the right shape to conceal a hard drive and the missing vials. What bothers me is how he got close enough to take Beacher out in the first place. Beacher was no fool. He wouldn't have stood by passively and let someone slit his throat."

"Is that what he was going to do to me?"

Gabriel's knuckles whitened on the steering wheel.

"I don't think your attacker in the parking lot was our killer. I think it was Andrea."

"Andrea!"

"Beacher said she followed him to Sunburst. What if she saw you coming out of my house that night?"

"You did ask if my attacker could have been a woman."

He nodded. "The person in the parking lot wore a hooded sweatshirt with a scarf over their face. Is that the same thing the person wore in your bedroom?"

The attack in the parking lot had been so sudden, but she saw what he was asking. "No. In my bedroom he wore…I'm not sure what it was exactly, but it wasn't a hooded sweatshirt. It reminded me of those ninja outfits in movies, but it still could have been the same person."

"Uh-huh, but let's say the attacker in the parking lot was Andrea. She might have returned later, but when you saw her and ran she couldn't know that you wouldn't call the police. Knowing her, I'd bet she cut her losses, went home and decided it was time to leave town."

Cassy considered. "That's a lot of supposition."

"But it fits."

"Maybe."

"The killer needed a reason to search your house."

"I did call Beacher several times and left messages.

He could have listened to one." If so, she'd led him right to her. "But why didn't he tear your house apart?"

"Because if I'd come home to a disaster I would have gone through the house with extreme caution."

"And spotted the trip wire."

"Exactly. He did search my house or it's unlikely he would have known about the gallery showing. I think he decided if he could kill me and blow up the toxin at the same time all his problems would be solved."

"Is that why he didn't slit your throat, too?"

"Maybe, but as everyone keeps pointing out, unlike Beacher, I have a well-earned reputation as a loner. I can't think of one person I'd let close enough to use a knife on me."

"Me."

He returned her smile with a wry twist of his lips. "You don't need a knife to do me in."

Chapter Twelve

Gabe pulled into a fast food drive-thru.

"I'm not hungry," Cassiopia protested.

"Neither am I, but there's no telling when we'll have time to stop again."

They ordered breakfast sandwiches and pulled over to eat without getting out of the car. She nibbled on hers without enthusiasm.

"I still don't see how he made the connection to that poor old woman last night."

"When he searched my house he would have seen that most of my work had been removed and the gallery invoice was sitting in plain sight on my desk."

"Then wouldn't he go to the gallery? And how would he know about Mrs. Morrison?"

"Who says he didn't go to the gallery?"

"I'm pretty sure someone would have noticed a hooded man dressed in black."

Gabe nearly smiled. "He didn't need to be hooded to walk into the gallery earlier in the day. No one there would know him as anything but a potential customer wanting to browse."

Cassiopia crumpled the paper that held her half-eaten sandwich.

"Either he was there when Mrs. Morrison bought the lion, or he heard Rochelle discussing its delivery."

"But why kill her and the poor man in the wheel-chair? Why not wait until they went to bed to break in?"

"The Morrison house had an alarm system. There was a sign out front. Given the neighborhood, he would know that alarm was likely being monitored."

"And the last thing he'd want is the police arriving," she agreed. "Still, why would she open the door to a masked...oh. He wasn't wearing his hood when he went to the door, was he? That's why he killed her."

"That's the way I have it figured. He's driving a Jaguar," Gabe continued. "Exactly the sort of car she would take for granted in that neighborhood."

"And not the sort of car your common criminal runs around in."

"No." Gabe crumpled his wrapper.

"What is it?"

"We need a pay phone."

"Why?"

Gabe gathered up the trash and dumped it without answering. He was still thinking through the ramifications. Calling Sliffman was dangerous, but not calling him might get someone else killed.

"You're going to call Sliffman, aren't you?" Cassiopia asked as he got back in and started the engine.

Gabe wasn't surprised that she'd followed his train of thought.

"Are you going to tell him what we found?"

Gabe hesitated, weighing the risks. Any admission

on his part could end up with him in jail unable to prove his innocence. "I don't know. I'm playing this by ear."

Cassiopia didn't press him, for which he was grateful. His mind was still sorting options, but one thing was clear—he needed to get to the gallery ahead of Rochelle.

"I have my cell phone," she offered.

Regretfully, he remembered the business card Sliffman had tried to hand him. "I don't have Sliffman's phone number."

"What's wrong with the police? I can phone in an anonymous tip that I saw a black Jaguar driving recklessly as it left her driveway last night. It will certainly get their attention."

Gabe was so used to being on his own he hadn't even considered calling the police for help. And, he admitted ruefully, he didn't want their help. He wanted to nail the bastard himself. But not badly enough to see another person die.

"Go ahead. They'll trace the call back to you, but they won't have our location."

Cassiopia bit at her lip then fished for her phone and turned it on. After trying for several seconds, she turned back to him in frustration.

"The battery's too low. I can't call out."

Gabe increased his speed.

"Why did he kill Andrea Fielding?"

"Remember Beacher's note? I think she knew or suspected who he was."

Cassiopia shook her head. "But if she was a threat now, she was a threat four years ago, wasn't she?"

"I don't know. Maybe he's just trying to get rid of loose ends."

"Like us."

"Yes."

"You're worried."

Gabe spared her a glance. "He was in a hurry last night. He didn't find anything and he's taking bigger and bigger risks."

"You think he'll try the gallery again this morning?"

"Yes."

"Oh! You think he'll hurt Rochelle."

"I think he'll hurt anyone who stands in his way."

"What's he going to do when he doesn't find the toxin?"

"Increase his efforts to find you."

"Me?"

As he stopped for a traffic light he held her gaze, knowing it was important that she understand the danger she represented.

"He needs to know what you told Beacher. He wants to know where that toxin is, Cassiopia."

"But I don't know!"

"Not specifically, but you told Beacher about your father using the exercise equipment. It's a good bet you were right about the toxin not leaving the building. Beacher made friends with someone who works there. I'm not sure how he talked his way inside, but you know his silver tongue."

"It was probably a woman."

He grinned. "You're probably right. As soon as we get to a phone you're going to call Sliffman to pick you up and place you in protective custody."

"Try again."

"Several people are already dead, Cassiopia. You're next on his list."

"You think I'd feel safe with the authorities babysitting me? People get killed all the time in protective custody."

"That's in the movies."

"So you say. I'm not willing to take that chance. What if Huntington is the one behind all this? No, thanks. I'm sticking with you. I know *you* won't let anything happen to me because I'd come back and haunt you forever."

He'd known she wouldn't agree and he didn't really want her someplace where he didn't know what was happening to her. "You'd do it, too."

"Believe it. What are you going to tell Rochelle Leeman?"

Gabe frowned. Since he couldn't be sure what Sliffman had told her the conversation would be tricky, but he needed to impress on her that she and her staff might be in danger.

"Shouldn't we also go see Dr. Pheng?" Cassiopia asked.

"Pheng won't talk to me. I've tried before."

"He'll talk to me."

Gabe didn't respond because they were coming up on the gallery. Being a Saturday morning, he'd made excellent time. The sleepy streets were just starting to wake with people and they still offered plenty of parking. He ignored the empty spaces and cruised slowly past the gallery. The light was hitting the display windows, but he thought he glimpsed a shadowy figure moving around inside.

He drove around to the delivery area. The store's

van and three cars were parked near the rear entrance. Rochelle's car wasn't there, but a black Jaguar with damage to the front fender was.

Gabe swore. It had the same license plate.

"Find a phone. Call the police."

He slammed the gearshift into Park and leapt out, running for the back door.

Locked.

Gabe pounded on its surface before sprinting around to the front of the building, drawing his gun as he ran.

HEART IN HER THROAT, Cassy watched Gabriel tear off. She climbed behind the wheel, but before she even settled in her seat, a hooded figure in black erupted from the back door and ran toward the Jaguar. In one hand, a long knife dripped splatters of blood. The opposite hand cradled a hefty-sized bronze animal on a wooden base.

Cassy froze long enough for the ninja to climb inside the Jag and start the engine. She pulled forward intending to block the other car, but the driver never hesitated. With a squeal of tires he plowed into her with enough force to shove her lighter car to one side and kept going.

Stunned, it took her a full second to realize the loud popping sounds were gunfire. Gabriel was sprinting toward her, a smoking weapon in his hand. He reached the car and flung open her door before she could move.

"Are you all right?"

"Yes."

"Stay here!"

GABE SPRINTED FOR the now open rear door of the building. Inside, a woman with dark hair sat on the floor of the workroom bent over a man. From the pungent, coppery scent of blood, Gabe knew what he'd find even before he approached the pair. The woman was making tiny broken sounds of distress.

"Rochelle!"

But it was Jennifer Mackley who lifted her head to stare at him without comprehension. Blood ran from a gash across her throat. Since it wasn't spurting, Gabe knew the artery hadn't been severed. That was probably due to the unconscious man on the floor.

There were obvious signs of a struggle. Spotting a bin of cloths they probably used to clean display pieces, he grabbed several and gently moved Jennifer to one side.

"Hold this against your throat."

Obediently, she pressed on the cloth he wrapped around her neck. Her eyes were wide and staring in shock.

Gabe turned his attention to the deliveryman Rochelle had called Dave. The large man was bleeding profusely from several wounds to his chest and abdomen and he was unconscious. His arrival may have saved Jennifer's life at the cost of his own.

Cassiopia ran inside and jerked to a stop. This was one time he was glad she hadn't listened to him.

"We need an ambulance."

She was already moving past him toward a wall phone near the door to the main room.

Gabe unzipped the man's jacket. Yanking up Dave's shirt, he used another cloth to apply pressure to the worst of the stab wounds.

"They're on the way," Cassiopia announced.

"Hold this," Gabe commanded. Her eyes were also wide, but her hands were steady as she took over for him. Jennifer had fallen silent. Gabe stood.

"Where are you going?"

"Get to Sliffman," Gabe told her. "He'll keep you safe."

"Get back here! Gabriel!"

He didn't answer. If he hurried, he still might catch the Jag and bring this nightmare to a close.

CASSY DECIDED she would throttle him at the earliest opportunity. Meantime, she was stuck. If she wasn't mistaken, the man on the floor was dying.

Abruptly, a large figure blocked the light as he stood silhouetted in the door's opening.

"What th—? Who are you? What's going on here?"

He wore jeans, not black pants, and he was much larger than the person she'd seen running from the building. He lumbered inside looking confused and annoyed.

"Go out front and let the paramedics in," she ordered.

"Is that Dave?"

"Yes." She didn't know if it was or not, but it didn't matter. "He's hurt. Hurry!"

The man swore then raced past her through the gallery to open the front door for the police and paramedics whose sirens shrilled out their approach.

Minutes later the room filled with people. Cassy was moved aside for the paramedics, but a uniformed police officer stopped her when she tried to leave.

"What happened here?"

"I don't know." She didn't have to fake the shrill tone

of her voice. She was quaking all over now that help had arrived. "A man dressed in black came running out the back door. I think it must have been a robbery. He was holding a knife and a statue. He jumped into a black-colored Jaguar and took off."

"A Jaguar?" the officer asked incredulously.

Cassy couldn't blame him, but she nodded wide-eyed. "The front fender was all smashed in. He left this door standing open so I looked inside. These poor people were bleeding all over."

"Take it easy. What's your name?"

"Janice Culpepper," she lied. "I work a couple of doors down. I used that phone on the wall to call for help."

"Did you get a good look at the man?"

"No. He was dressed like a ninja."

"A ninja?"

She bobbed her head. "Like in those movies where they dress all in black and know karate and stuff."

"Okay. Wait over there please, miss." She heard him mutter under his breath, "A ninja and a Jaguar," before he turned to the big man who was crowding the ambulance attendants in his concern over his friend. "Sir, you're going to have to stand back and let the paramedics work."

"But that's Dave! Is he gonna die?"

Cassy inched toward the back door again. People had begun to gather as the shopkeepers arrived for the start of their business day. Rochelle Leeman pushed her way inside.

"What's going on here?"

"Ma'am, you'll have to step outside."

"This is my gallery! What happened here? Good

God, is that Dave? And Jennifer?" She moved toward them with admirable speed. "What happened?"

While the police officer's attention was on her, Cassy stepped outside. She walked away quickly shaking her head and muttering, "Horrible," for the benefit of those clustered near the door.

No one stopped her. She hoped the officer would assume she'd returned to her own shop. That would buy her a couple of minutes before he raised a hue and cry.

As soon as she rounded the corner she broke into a run and crossed the street. Her purse banged against her side. She didn't even remember taking it from the car. She'd jammed her sling inside on top but if she was stopped and searched, she'd have a hard time explaining why she had a box with a government classified hard drive in her purse.

She would kill Gabriel for leaving her stranded like this. *She* wasn't carrying a nice fat envelope full of cash. Her wallet contained a little over twenty dollars. And her hand was sticky with blood. Great. Just great.

He would suffer when she found him again. A slow death, she promised herself. She rubbed her hand on her slacks in an effort to wipe the blood away.

Her teeth were chattering, but she didn't have time for hysterics. What would happen if Gabriel did catch up with the Jag? The ninja could have a gun as well as a knife. And Cassy needed to get off the street before the police started looking for her. But where could she go?

A horn honked sharply and repeatedly. Cassy glanced around. Gabriel was blocking traffic on the opposite side of the street, motioning to her.

An SUV nearly ran her over as she crossed to reach

the car. The passenger door was dented shut from its impact with the Jag, but she was able to get the back door open. The minute she was inside, Gabe pulled away from the curb.

"I could kill you!" she yelled.

"Later."

Police were fanning out from the side street. Cassy lay down across the backseat, pretending she was invisible. "Get us out of here."

"Workin' on it."

"Work faster! Why'd you come back?"

"It's Saturday."

No matter how she thought about that, she couldn't derive any sense from his statement. "So?"

"Even Sliffman gets days off. You would have spent a lot of time answering questions from people whose reactions I can't predict before someone actually called him."

"And you were going to do what? Sacrifice yourself to get me out of there?"

"No. I'd have thought of something, but you got yourself out of there. You can sit up now."

"What are we going to do?"

"Retrieve the toxin, talk to Dr. Pheng and take everything we have to Sliffman."

Cassy shook her head. "How do we get inside Sunburst? Even if we do, we still don't know exactly where to look."

"True."

"People are being killed, Gabriel. We need to talk to Sliffman first."

He pursed his lips but nodded. "Sliffman it is. We need a telephone book."

But when they located a phone book they discovered Sliffman wasn't listed. Huntington was.

"We're going to his home?" Cassy asked in surprise when Gabriel told her what he intended. "Is that wise? What if he's the one behind all this?"

"There's only one way to find out. Don't worry, I'll take some precautions. He won't risk killing us in his own home."

"Are you sure about that?"

"You want to wait while I see him alone?"

Yes! "No."

"Then what choice do we have?"

GABE STARED AT the modest house in the Frederick suburbs as he parked across the street. A brand-new green Lexus sat in front. The garage door was open and a pair of shiny new bicycles leaned against the wall inside. Two young girls spilled from the house and went running across the lawn.

Gabe had known Huntington was married, he just hadn't expected the dour major to have a young family.

Huntington himself appeared and began moving around in the garage. Gabe had never seen him dressed in civilian clothing before. He was never going to like the man, but it made him more human somehow.

"I don't suppose you'll wait here in the car?" he asked Cassiopia.

"Good guess." She bit uneasily at her bottom lip. "Maybe we should wait until we can reach Sliffman."

"We can't afford to wait."

Gabe slipped his gun into his hand. "If this goes wrong. Leave."

"You can't shoot him!"

"No. As tempting as it might be, this is to keep him from getting ideas about shooting me."

Cassiopia looked as if she were going to object further, but Huntington had pulled what appeared to be a new lawnmower onto the driveway. Gabe stepped from the car as he began to fill it with gasoline. Huntington looked up. Shock stiffened his spine. Gabe let him see the gun and watched fear send his gaze roving in search of his children.

"I don't plan to use it," Gabe told him.

"What are you doing here?"

"We need to talk."

Huntington's gaze went to Cassiopia, who spoke quickly.

"We have something to tell you. Please give us a chance."

Gabe kept his eyes on Huntington. "Two civilians were murdered last night. Two others were attacked this morning."

Huntington narrowed his eyes as Cassiopia moved to stand at Gabe's side. "They were killed by the same person who murdered Beacher Coyle and Andrea Fielding."

"Why?"

"Because someone believes Beacher found the toxin," he told the man.

"Did he?"

Gabe ignored the question. "I told Sliffman to look

at Andrea's brother." He watched Huntington's gaze narrow. "Did he?" For a long minute, Gabe thought he wouldn't get an answer in return, but Huntington finally gave an abrupt nod.

"The brother got drunk and fell to his death in a parking garage in D.C.," Huntington told him grudgingly. "His former girlfriend disappeared in Chicago. His best friend died in an apparent robbery. Another one committed suicide while another OD'd on drugs."

"All neat and tidy. Was the one who died in a robbery stabbed?" Gabe read the answer on the major's stern face. "Our killer likes knives. He's had combat training."

"Come inside. We'll discuss this."

"I like it here."

Huntington scowled. "You always did have a problem with authority."

"Yep, and you're a military man." The scowl deepened. "Pheng's ex-military, isn't he?"

"What do you want, Lowe?" The low growl was a warning.

"Have Carstairs exhumed."

That broke through Huntington's stoic facade. "He had a heart condition!"

"And everyone knew it. With access to the right drugs…" Gabe let him fill in the blank. "Think it was coincidence he died that same night?"

"You're still suggesting the major was involved in the theft?"

"He had access to the vault." Gabe allowed a tiny shrug. "He also had access to the missing explosive."

"So did you."

"And you," Gabe agreed, "but Carstairs left the

base during the doctor's missing hours, and someone sent me to the Richards house that night."

"You still maintain you don't remember?"

"I'd like nothing better than to remember."

Huntington's scowl was fierce. "Those orders would have come through me."

"Yes, sir. I made a convenient scapegoat, didn't I?"

"Spit it out, Lowe. You think I was involved?"

"Were you?"

Huntington swore.

"Nice new lawnmower. The Lexus looks new, too. Hit the lottery did you?"

For a second, Gabe thought the man would swing at him. Huntington kept his fists at his side with obvious effort.

"My wife's mother died, you little bastard."

"Sorry to hear it. She must have been loaded. That will make losing your promotion a whole lot easier to take, won't it?"

Cassiopia interrupted before the major forgot Gabriel had a gun and went for his throat. "Gabriel did not kill my father."

Watching Huntington control his temper was enlightening.

"I see you made a convert," he snarled. "Why civilians?"

"Someone thinks I have the toxin," Gabe told him.

"Do you?"

"No."

Cassiopia interrupted once again. "We think my dad took the toxin and the research to protect me."

"Where's your proof?"

"Have her mother's body exhumed as well as Carstairs," Gabe suggested.

Cassiopia drew in a sharp breath. "Gabe! She was cremated. You don't think—?"

"The killer needed leverage against your father," he explained without looking away from Huntington. "Telling your dad that your mother was murdered, whether she was or not, would give your father a strong incentive to protect you."

Huntington muttered under his breath.

"Dad still wouldn't have given the toxin to anyone," Cassiopia objected.

Gabe nodded. "He didn't. He pulled a switch and gave Carstairs a fake. By the time the person behind this realized what he'd done, Carstairs and your father were dead and he didn't have what he wanted."

Huntington stiffened.

"Carstairs was career military," Gabe continued. "He was going to be cashiered out because of his heart condition. Maybe he was promised money to retire in style. Maybe the killer had something on him. The motive doesn't matter. Once Carstairs sent me to the Richards' place and turned over what Dr. Richards gave him, Carstairs's usefulness was over. The authorities would focus on me while the killer cleaned up loose ends."

Huntington's eyes narrowed dangerously. "That's quite a tale you're spinning."

"Isn't it?" Gabe agreed.

"It makes terrifying sense, Major," Cassiopia put in. "Andrea's brother and his friends were loose ends."

"Why?"

"Backup scapegoats," Gabe answered.

Huntington huffed out a breath. When he spoke, it was grudgingly. "We looked into them before."

"And now they're all dead," Gabe reminded him.

"Let's go inside." It was an order.

Gabe stiffened. "As you've pointed out, I've got a problem with authority. The toxin is still at Sunburst."

"The place was searched," he argued coldly.

"Search again." He grabbed Cassiopia's good arm when she would have added something. "We're leaving."

He thought she'd argue but Huntington started to step around the lawnmower and Gabe flashed his gun in warning. The approach of two giggling little girls stopped Huntington in his tracks. Fury and the promise of retribution filled his expression.

Chapter Thirteen

Cassy allowed Gabe to hustle her toward the street, but once there, she yanked her arm free, furious with his high-handed antics.

"Why didn't you tell him about the gym?" she demanded as soon as they were in the car. "You told him everything else."

Gabe had them moving down the street before he answered. Huntington had vanished inside while the little girls claimed their bicycles from the open garage.

"If he's the killer, he already knew everything else," Gabe answered.

"Do you really think he's the killer?"

"He didn't ask the right questions."

"What are you talking about?"

"He asked *why* civilians, not *which* civilians. How did he know who I was talking about?"

She thought about that.

"Huntington gets off on authority. Until I know for sure we aren't misreading what we do know, I'm not going to trust that son of a bitch."

"Then why did we go there?"

Gabe shot her an unreadable look. "To add a piece to the puzzle."

"Okay, I missed that. What did we add?"

"That depends on what Huntington does with the information we just gave him. If he calls Sliffman, he's innocent. If he goes to Sunburst alone, he isn't."

"Oh."

Gabe smiled without humor. "What you don't know, because the information was never made public, is that the hard drive and toxin aren't the only things missing. Other classified drives were stolen from the base at the same time."

"What else was taken?"

"I don't know, and couldn't tell you if I did, but all of the existing toxin along with every scrap of data pertaining to it is gone. That isn't true for the other items, but a person who didn't know the system wouldn't have known for sure which hard drive went with the toxin."

"You think Huntington took them and sold them?"

"Actually, I always thought Carstairs took them."

"Could either of them simply walk off the base with a stack of classified hard drives?"

"Nope. But someone did."

She released a deep breath. "This just gets more and more complicated."

"Welcome to my world. Huntington was transferred a few months after the theft. He was reassigned to the base just recently. I wish we could run a check on his mother-in-law to see exactly what sort of inheritance she left her daughter."

"Is that what we're going to do now?"

"No. First we'll see if my bike is still there and in

drivable condition. Then we'll have a go at Dr. Pheng.
I'd give a lot to know what the doctor had to say to
Beacher about Andrea."

Cassy fastened on the words that brought her brain
to a halt. "Your bike?"

His expression was not reassuring. "I want an alter-
native form of transportation available."

"Rent another car," she demanded. "That bike isn't
an option."

"It's not raining," he pointed out.

"I don't care. It's a deathtrap on wheels. I am not
riding on it again."

"That's okay, you can use the car."

DR. PHENG OWNED a stately home in a pricey section of
town. He lived with his wife, his mother, one of two
grown sons, his daughter-in-law and two grandchil-
dren. The artistically landscaped grounds held an im-
pressively large fountain, which graced the lawn in
front of a covered portico flanked by roman columns.
A pair of elegantly cut wooden doors and two urns of
flowers guarded the opening. A number of expensive-
looking vehicles filled the curved driveway. None of
them was a black Jaguar, but Dr. Pheng was obviously
entertaining.

Cassy waited for Gabe to climb off his death
machine and join her. It was unfortunate that the bike
had only sustained cosmetic damage. She'd seriously
hoped it had been damaged beyond repair, stolen or
towed away.

"Maybe we should wait. It looks like he has company." A whiff of burning charcoal told her why.

"All the better. Come on." They started up the long driveway. "Impressive," Gabe allowed, staring at the large, white structure.

"Old family money," she told him.

"Obviously. He didn't buy this on a research chemist's salary."

"No. His mother actually owns the house. Her family is quite wealthy. Textiles, I think. Dr. Pheng's only daughter married a pediatrician. His oldest son is a successful importer. The son that lives with them is studying to be a lawyer and he's got a brother who's a cardiologist, another brother who's a respected mathematician and a sister who's a seismologist."

"You seem to know a lot about the family."

"Christmas cards over the years," she explained. "Dr. Pheng comes from a long line of successful overachievers. My dad told me he and Dr. Pheng were always competing with one another in school for top honors."

"Who won?"

Cassy grinned. "He never said, but they remained friendly adversaries."

Gabriel didn't return her smile. "Let me direct the conversation, okay?"

"Why?"

"You're too trusting."

That shocked her. "You don't trust Dr. Pheng? It was his research that was stolen!"

"I don't trust anyone."

"Thanks a lot."

His features softened. "You're the exception."

"That's better, but don't you think you're being a little paranoid?"

"Yes."

At least the man knew his faults. "Okay. You're in charge."

His grin was fleeting, but genuine. "Bet that cost you. Come on."

Cassy didn't know whether to laugh or hit him, but her nerves took over as they approached the expensive double doors. "I still think we should wait and come back."

"Too late," Gabe pointed out as he pressed the fancy doorbell.

A young woman answered the soft chime a few minutes later.

"Yes?"

"Dr. Cassiopia Richards and Gabriel Lowe to see Dr. Pheng," he told the woman.

"Oh." Her puzzled features frowned. "Is he expecting you?"

"No, ma'am, but it's important or we wouldn't bother him on a Saturday evening."

"Please, come inside. He's out back. We're having a family barbeque."

"This will only take a few minutes," he assured her.

She did not look happy. "One moment, please."

They were left standing in an impressive foyer of marble and gilt. Overdone for Cassy's taste, but she had no doubt the marble inlay table alone cost a fortune. The centerpiece was a profusion of yellow roses in an exquisitely cut lead crystal vase.

For a house where there were a number of people, it was oddly silent. Cassy looked at Gabriel. His expression was unreadable as he watched Dr. Pheng stride down the hall toward them.

The doctor had aged considerably since Cassy had seen him last. His hair was mostly white now, his features lined. His expression was inscrutable as he ignored Gabriel and walked straight toward her.

"Ms. Richards, it's been a long time."

He hadn't used her title. Normally that wouldn't have bothered her, but Cassy felt certain the slight was deliberate. She had no idea why, but there was something cold in his manner. She reminded herself they were the intruders here and interrupting a family gathering. Besides, she might be misreading him completely.

"Hello, doctor. I believe you know Gabriel Lowe."

"Yes."

Just that. The two men faced one another like opponents seeking a weakness.

"Beacher Coyle came to see you," Gabriel began. "Will you tell us what was said?"

"Why?"

"Because he's dead. We believe he discovered where your missing toxin went."

"Then you should be speaking with the authorities."

"Doctor, please," she interrupted. "Gabriel had nothing to do with what happened four years ago. He's trying to help."

"Even if I believed that, Ms. Richards, there is nothing he can do."

"You're wrong."

Gabriel squeezed her arm in warning without lifting his gaze from the doctor. "Beacher left me a note. He said he planned to talk to you about Andrea Fielding. We're fairly certain she was involved in the theft."

"Then you know more than I. Ms. Fielding was a barely competent lab assistant."

"Whose brother disliked your form of research," Gabriel added just as coldly.

"I know nothing about her family or her personal life. I have told the authorities everything many times. Despite the fact that I have moved on they continue to badger me. I can't help you."

Cassy found it hard not to feel angry with him here in his ostentatious home. "You mean, you won't."

"If you wish to put it harshly, yes."

Her anger rose. "Your life wasn't the only one affected by what happened."

"I regret the death of your father, Ms. Richards."

She realized to her shock that she'd been thinking of Gabriel, not her father.

"It's *Dr.* Richards," she told him evenly. Gabriel touched her arm, but she ignored him. "I'd think you'd be jumping at the chance to help us recover your data."

"I no longer work for the military. The data belongs to them, not me. I'm sorry, but I told Mr. Coyle exactly what I'm telling you."

There was a ring of truth to his words.

"Now if you'll excuse me, my family and guests are waiting." He held open the front door in clear dismissal.

Cassy fumed while Gabriel's expression remained neutral as he stepped outside. "One last thing, doctor. Do you know anyone who owns a black Jaguar?"

The man didn't blink or hesitate. "Yes. Several people. Good day. I'm sorry I couldn't be of more assistance."

"No," Cassy told him bluntly. "You aren't."

Seething, she strode toward the battered car without looking back.

"That arrogant, uncaring…how can he be so, so… awful?"

"Because he's lying."

Cassy stopped dead. Gabriel climbed astride his motorcycle. He was looking toward the closed front door of the big house.

"How do you know?"

"Intuition. Follow me."

"Do I salute first?"

His lips curved slightly. "Only if you want. Sorry, but we shouldn't stand here talking."

"Fine." Fuming, she turned back to the car. Gabriel's arrogant manner wasn't intended to get her back up, but she was nervous. And scared. And her wrist throbbed despite the tablets she'd swallowed this morning. Unfortunately, she couldn't put her arm back in the sling and still drive.

When Gabriel pulled off the road a short distance later, she pulled in behind him. He came to stand at her open window. "We need a look inside his garage."

"You can't be serious."

"Picture him in black. Is he the right size to be your ninja?"

Her heart began to thud heavily. "Why would you even think such a thing? You're talking murder here, Gabe. The man is a respected scientist. And what would be his motive?"

"I don't know, but do you know anyone else who was involved four years ago that can afford to drive around in a black Jaguar?"

"No." Fear rose up, threatening to choke her. "You can't go back there! He's got a house full of people!"

"Relax. I'm not going back right now."

She couldn't possibly relax. "I thought it was Huntington you didn't trust."

"I don't. Did you notice the shiny new Lexus in *his* driveway? Could *he* have been the man you saw?"

Trying to picture the officious major in a ninja outfit was impossible. "I don't know. Both men are thin."

"Dr. Pheng is considerably shorter. And he was wearing a pair of black pants just now."

The major had been dressed in jeans.

"That doesn't mean anything. They both had plenty of time to change clothing."

He waited.

"I just don't know."

"Okay. We rattled their cages. The Jag has major damage now and the driver knows we can identify it. His first step will be to get the Jag out of sight."

"Won't he try to have it repaired?"

"Repairs can be traced. Unless your ninja knows a chop shop, he's got an expensive liability on his hands."

"Maybe the Jag was stolen."

"Undoubtedly it will be reported that way."

"That alone would tell us, won't it?"

"Sure. If he doesn't kill us first."

"Thank you. You've just made a bad day perfect."

"I WON'T LET THAT HAPPEN," Gabe promised.

Her smile held the slightest wobble. "Of course not. You're just trying to scare me. Congratulations, I'm scared. What do we do now?"

"Do you think you can get us in to Sunburst Labs?"

"Sure. No problem. Do you want a tour of the White House, too?" Her sarcasm edged on hysteria. "I don't have those sort of connections."

"Relax. You know the people who worked with your father."

"A number of them, yes, but they can't just take me in to a secured lab on a Saturday evening. What am I supposed to tell them?"

"Let's try the truth. We passed a phone booth at that gas station back there. Let's go."

Cassiopia's look plainly said she thought he'd lost his mind, but she followed him back to the gas station and waited while he fished for change and called information to get Arthur Longstreet's number.

"You're going to call the head of security at Sunburst Labs?" she asked, when he disconnected.

"No, you are. Tell him you suspect your father left the missing toxin inside the building and you've thought of a place where it might be."

"He'll tell me to call Homeland Security."

"Fine. Get him to give you Sliffman's phone number."

"Why do I think this is a really bad idea?"

Gabe shrugged. "It's all I have unless you want to go back and stand watch while I break into Pheng's garage."

"Pass."

"We can't keep running and hiding in motel rooms."

"I like motel rooms. You don't even hog the blankets."

He grinned as she reached for the phone and punched in the number he gave her.

"See if he'll meet us at the lab."

She rolled her eyes and began speaking as someone on the other end answered.

"This is Dr. Cassiopia Richards. I wonder if I might speak with Arthur Longstreet? Yes, I will. Thank you." She didn't look at Gabe as she waited. "Mr. Longstreet? I don't know if you remember me… Yes, it has been. I'm sorry to trouble you on a Saturday, but I wonder if I could have a few minutes of your time this evening."

She forced excitement into her voice.

"I think I know what may have happened to the missing toxin…. Yes, I know, but I'd rather call the authorities *after* we see if I'm right. I'll feel pretty foolish if I'm wrong. I'm not far from Sunburst right now…. Uh-huh. Yes, I do…. I know, but I'd rather not go into detail on the phone. This won't take long if I'm right. I know it's a huge imposition…. Yes. Thank you. I'll wait for you there."

She disconnected with a mixed expression. "He's going to meet me in the parking lot."

"Excellent."

"What if we're wrong?"

"What if we're right?" he countered.

"I'm scared."

He bent and covered her mouth. Her lips were incredibly soft but receptive as he kissed some warmth back into them.

"I'm scared, too," he agreed gently, "but I promise I won't let anything happen to you."

"I know. I won't let anything happen to you, either."

He smiled because he could see she was serious. "You're an easy person to care about, Cassiopia. Let's go." Before he did or said something utterly stupid.

He climbed on the bike while worry hammered at him. Would Longstreet show or would he have the authorities meet them there? Gabe wished he could have left Cassiopia out of this. Despite his promise, something could go horribly wrong and he was ill-prepared to protect her.

As he pulled into the parking lot of Sunburst Laboratories Gabe spotted security cameras positioned around the building and tried to relax. Whatever came next, he'd be just as happy to have on camera.

Cassiopia joined him and he slid his arm around her shoulders. Her hand circled his waist. Neither of them spoke as they waited beneath an electric light pole.

Arthur Longstreet should have been tall and thin given his name, but he wasn't either one. As the beefy man stepped from his midsized sedan, Gabe watched the experienced ex-cop approach them cautiously. He remembered Longstreet. The man was older now, but still fit and alert. He took his job and his responsibilities seriously.

He recognized Gabe and he did not look surprised. That gave Gabe a measure of hope as he approached them with wary confidence.

"Dr. Richards?"

Cassiopia stepped forward. "Thank you for coming. You remember Gabriel Lowe?"

"Yes. You're looking pretty lively for a dead man."

Gabe inclined his head. "Right house, wrong victim," he agreed. Longstreet didn't offer to shake hands and neither did he.

"As I told you on the phone, Mr. Longstreet, we think we know where my father put the missing toxin."

"You didn't mention Mr. Lowe."

Gabe answered for her. "I was afraid you wouldn't come if she did."

"Gabriel was as much a victim as my father was," Cassiopia told him stoutly. "The only way to prove that is to find the toxin. Please help us. I know Sunburst has been searched repeatedly, but what about the gym? I'm not talking about the locker room, I'm talking about the room with all the equipment."

"There isn't anyplace in there to hide something."

"I think you're wrong. My father liked to work out on his lunch hour. The one place no one would expect to find something like the toxin is in an open gym."

Longstreet continued to look skeptical. "Dr. Richards, we've been over the building repeatedly."

"Humor me. Please?"

"Beacher Coyle already found the toxin here at Sunburst," Gabe told him. "He left me a note saying he left it here because he was afraid to remove it."

"Beacher Coyle is dead."

"Yes, he is," Gabe agreed. "And his murderer wants Cassiopia and me dead as well. Show him the hard drive in your purse."

"Gabe!" she protested.

At the same time, Longstreet stiffened. His hand went to his jacket pocket. "Hold still, Dr. Richards. Keep your hands were I can see them. Both of you."

As he pulled a gun, Gabe nodded, unperturbed. "I'm armed, too," he told the man. "You can have the gun, but understand that someone has already tried to kill us."

Moving slowly and keeping his hands clear, Gabe took the position against the battered car. Trusting

Longstreet was a risk, but the man was built wrong to be Cassiopia's ninja.

"There's a gun in my purse, too," she offered.

Gabe wished she'd kept silent about that.

"Set the bag on the ground and turn and face the car like Mr. Lowe."

Longstreet was thorough. He removed Gabe's gun and stepped back before turning to Cassiopia's purse. He took her gun as well but didn't touch the hard drive although he eyed it for several seconds.

"Any other surprises?" Longstreet demanded.

"No, but I'd feel a whole lot more comfortable inside than standing out here in the open."

With a quick glance around, Longstreet nodded agreement.

There were security cameras, locks to be swiped, a metal detector to walk through and an armed man at the reception desk. Longstreet signed them in, issued them temporary badges and told the guard to have someone named Jason meet them at the gym.

Jason proved to be a tall black man with ex-military in his carriage who eyed Gabe and Cassiopia with alert curiosity. Longstreet didn't bother with introductions and Jason opened the gym door, turned on the lights and stepped to one side.

It wasn't a large space but it was comfortably packed with all sorts of exercise equipment. One wall was covered in a bank of floor-to-ceiling windows. The grounds outside were dark enough that Gabe could barely make out the building addition across the court-yard from them.

"What are we looking for?" Longstreet asked.

"Space where a person could stow a package about this big," Gabe replied, indicating the size with his hands.

"In here?" Jason asked skeptically.

"Look for loose tiles, panels, flooring, whatever. What was your father's favorite equipment, Cassiopia?"

"I don't know. He used the bike and treadmill, but probably everything else in here as well."

"We'll start with them first. How often is this stuff moved for cleaning?" Gabe asked.

Longstreet looked grim. "Let's find out."

"Wait a minute. What about up there?" Cassiopia pointed toward the cold air return high up on the ceiling.

"Why there?" Longstreet asked.

"Dad would have wanted someplace simple and quick that wasn't apt to be examined by anyone," Cassiopia explained. "He always carried one of those all-purpose knives. You know the kind with enough heads that you can build a house from scratch?"

"There's a ladder in the storage closet," Jason told his boss.

"Bring it."

"Brilliant," Gabe told her.

She flushed, but demurred. "Wait until we see if I'm right."

Jason brought the ladder and positioned it beneath the opening. It turned out that he also carried one of those all-purpose knives, suitable for removing screws. Longstreet stopped him as he started up the ladder.

"Hold it, Jason. Dr. Richards, if the toxin is there, does it need special handling?"

"It should be in some sort of safety container. Just don't drop it."

"But no pressure, right?" Jason's smile was wry as he continued up the ladder. "This thing's been opened recently," he told them, removing the loosened screws that held it in place.

"Beacher," Cassiopia and Gabe said at the same time.

Jason removed the grate and passed it down. Pulling a flashlight from his belt, he shined it around inside. "I'll be darned. There's a case of some kind up here."

Gabe flashed her a grin. "Brilliant."

Cassiopia smiled back.

"Bring it down carefully, Jason," Longstreet ordered.

"Yes, sir."

When he would have handed the case to Longstreet, the security man indicated Cassiopia should take it. Inside were three vials marked with serial numbers. The clear liquid that filled them could have been anything at all. Gabe handed the grill back up for Jason to replace.

At the sound of a shot, Gabe flattened Cassiopia against the floor behind the stationary bike. A volley of shots followed the first through one of the windows. The case lid went flying as she fell, still clutching the case itself. Arthur Longstreet collapsed to the floor beside them. Blood spurted from a wound in his chest.

"Stay down!" Gabe yelled. He crawled to the man's side. Longstreet was clawing for his weapon. Abruptly, the room plunged into darkness. Jason had cut the lights. Gabe hoped the man had tripped the alarm as well if the broken window hadn't already.

Longstreet shoved his gun at Gabe. The older man's breathing was labored. Blood bubbled at the corner of his mouth. Gabe guessed the bullet had caught a lung.

"Stay still," he whispered. Cassiopia crawled over to him as the barrage of shots continued.

"The door. Get help."

The large window collapsed, sending shards of glass everywhere.

Chapter Fourteen

With the case of vials clutched protectively in her bad hand, Cassy tried to crawl along the floor toward the door. Her fingers encountered human flesh. The man called Jason was sprawled on the tile floor and he didn't move under her touch. In the dark, she couldn't tell how badly he was injured, but she felt the sticky warmth of blood seeping from somewhere.

Horrified, she tried to go around him, but his body was blocking the entrance. Unexpectedly, everything went eerily silent. Cassy bit back Gabriel's name and stilled.

Glass crunched underfoot. She didn't need light to know the gunman was inside with them.

Sudden flame licked the blackness as someone fired again. The room erupted in another barrage of shots that pinged off the metal equipment. Cassy tried to make herself as small as possible. There was a thud and the room went still once more. Terrified, she waited.

Someone shoved against the door from the hall outside. Jason's body pushed against her as the light flooded the immediate opening. Another burst of gunfire and another body fell, this time in the hall outside. The door swung closed.

Running footsteps came within feet of her. The overhead lights came on as the gunman located the wall switch. Cassy stared up at her hooded ninja and the gun gripped firmly in his hand.

"Give it to me," he demanded.

She knew that voice. "Dr. Pheng?"

The gun vanished. He dove at Cassy. There was no time to move. He yanked her hair and lifted her head up and back to expose her neck. A large knife appeared in his hand. She felt the blade bite her skin and stilled.

"I will kill her," he promised. "Drop your weapon."

Gabriel was on his feet, his weapon aimed at them. Blood ran down the side of his face. He didn't seem to notice.

"Drop it," Pheng ordered once more.

"That's not how it works."

"Then she dies."

Gabriel shook his head and swayed. "No. No one else dies."

The knife bit deeper. She felt blood well and begin to trickle down her neck. The case containing the vials dropped from her numb hand. Two rolled harmlessly toward Gabriel. The third hit metal and broke open.

Cassy gasped in horror. Dr. Pheng released her to toss his knife at Gabriel. He ducked and the room erupted in more gunfire. But these shots came from the shattered window.

Dr. Pheng jerked as a bullet slammed into his shoulder. Gabriel lunged for him. Major Huntington erupted through the shattered window, gun in hand. He was not alone.

"Get back!" Cassy yelled at them. "The toxin's been spilled!"

Everyone stopped moving except Gabriel and Dr. Pheng. Gabriel smashed his gun against the side of the other man's head. At the same time, Cassy scrambled to stop Longstreet's blood from reaching the spilled liquid. She was too late. Blood mingled with the toxin.

Horrified, she drew in a breath and held it, knowing it was futile. They were already dead.

"Get a containment unit in here!" Huntington yelled.

Cassy expelled her breath. "It's too late." But she didn't feel any differently. They should already be dead. Why weren't they dead?

Gabriel moved to her side. "How bad are you hurt?"

She touched her neck where the warm slide of blood was flowing down her throat. "It's a scratch."

"Why aren't we dead?"

She shook her head. The cut began to throb. "I don't know. Maybe it's inert in blood."

Huntington yanked the mask from Dr. Pheng's face. The doctor faced him with angry eyes. Huntington pulled out a pair of handcuffs and yanked his arms behind his back.

"Why aren't we dead, doctor?" he asked the man.

Dr. Pheng smiled coldly.

GABE WALKED OUT OF the wreckage of his house for the last time carrying the plastic box he'd been using all morning to collect the few items he'd been able to salvage from the burned-out shell. This time, it held the miraculously intact rosebush sculpture.

He should have been surprised to see Cassiopia

standing beside his truck, but he wasn't. He'd known she wouldn't let him put her off forever, but he wished she didn't look so unbelievably lovely standing there.

"It wasn't ruined!" she exclaimed as he placed the open box on the floor in the back of his truck.

"The kiln protected it," he explained.

"I'm glad. I hated thinking it had been destroyed."

The moment was as awkward as he'd known it was going to be.

"You've been avoiding me."

He saw no point denying the obvious.

"Why?"

"I've been busy. And it looks like I'm not done yet."

She followed as he inclined his head toward the street where a car was pulling up to the curb. Sliffman and Huntington stepped out and strode toward them. Gabe hadn't spoken to either one since his release from the lab more than a week ago.

Hazmat teams had isolated Sunburst, and the people exposed, for days while they tried to contain, assess and clean up the damage. A team of doctors had been brought in to treat the wounded while a team of scientists tried to determine why the toxin hadn't reacted with the blood. No one had become ill or showed any signs of contamination.

Cassiopia moved to Gabe's side in a show of solidarity that warmed the cold places inside him, while at the same time making him wish for the impossible.

"Lowe," Sliffman greeted. "Dr. Richards."

Cassiopia stiffened. "What do you want now?"

Gabe touched her in warning.

Huntington's scowl deepened, but Sliffman only

smiled. "We come bearing information, not asking more questions. A preliminary report is being pulled together right now and we felt you deserve to know the results of the findings. This information is not for public dissemination, however."

"The toxin?" Cassiopia asked.

Sliffman's lips pursed and he shook his head. "There was no toxin, Dr. Richards. Dr. Pheng faked the whole thing."

"What are you talking about? How do you fake a deadly toxin?"

"*Why* would he fake it?" Gabe demanded.

"Did he tell you this?" Cassiopia asked anxiously.

"Pheng won't be telling anyone anything," Huntington told them. "The sneaky little bastard managed to slit his wrists. The how is being looked into. Someone's head is going to roll over that."

Cassiopia made a small sound of distress. Gabe glared at him. "Did he talk?"

It was Sliffman who answered. "No. He never said a word to anyone. We've made a few assumptions based on what we do know. Four years ago the base was making cuts in outside contractors. Dr. Pheng held a senior position at the lab, but it was felt that his work could be absorbed by other, lower-paid scientists there."

"He was being fired?" Gabe asked.

"More or less. His research projects were going nowhere despite pressure to produce results."

"He was an overachiever, Gabe," Cassiopia inserted. "His reputation was everything."

"Too true, doctor. He must have guessed his name was on the list when several vials of an unidentified substance were sent to him for a priority analysis. I'm not at liberty to tell you where the vials came from or anything about them. Suffice to say there was a great deal of new pressure to determine what the substance was."

"He told them it was some new, deadly toxin," Huntington added.

Cassiopia shook her head in denial. "He lied?"

"Yes, doctor," Sliffman agreed. "As near as we can determine, he lied. Not only did he assure those in command that the toxin was a massive threat, he convinced them that with a little time he could come up with an antidote that would counter its effects."

"I don't believe it," she protested. "He had to know he'd be found out."

"That's why he set out to make everything disappear, including all his research."

Huntington laughed without humor. "The cold bastard was actually negotiating for a new job with his current employers while he set up the whole thing."

"Unfortunately for Dr. Pheng, a peer review was arranged before he was ready to implement his plan. We believe he intended for the theft to happen before the toxin was sent to your father. It appears that Ms. Fielding, her brother and his friends were initially supposed to take the blame when everything disappeared."

"How did he manage to clear out the vault?"

Huntington looked pained. "We can't discuss that."

"But," Sliffman added, "we believe your assumption about Major Carstairs was correct. When the timetable was moved up plans had to change quickly. Dr. Richards couldn't be allowed to complete his examination of the toxin or Dr. Pheng's research."

"For my father to be the one to uncover his hoax would have been intolerable," Cassiopia agreed.

Sliffman nodded, but Huntington's expression was hard. "The guy was a nut case."

Cassiopia shook her head sadly. "He wasn't insane, Major. His culture would demand that he not lose face."

"Even if he had to kill a lot of people?" the major grumped.

Her eyes clouded. "Even then. I don't excuse him. No one can. But I'm not surprised he killed himself. I'm just grateful that thanks to your timely arrival, we weren't numbered among his victims and neither were Mr. Longstreet or his coworker."

"How *did* you arrive in the nick of time?" Gabe asked.

Huntington grinned. "You called Longstreet, he called his boss, his boss called Sliffman—"

"And I called the major," Sliffman completed.

"I never liked you, Lowe. I still don't, but I do owe you an apology."

"We owe you our lives. I'd say that makes us even."

After a moment, Huntington nodded.

Cassiopia slipped her cold hand into Gabe's. He clasped it gently. "Is it over?" she asked.

"Yes, as far as the government is concerned." Sliffman handed her his business card. "We just wanted you to know. Best of luck to both of you."

"Thanks for telling us."

Silently, Gabe watched them return to their car. The crisp, fall afternoon cast sharp shadows on the ground. For the first time in a long time, he didn't have the urge to stand in one of them.

Cassiopia inhaled and exhaled deeply before turning to look up at him, when he dropped her hand. "New beginnings are good. Speaking of which, that's a new look for you, isn't it?"

Gabe ran his hand over his clean-shaven head. He'd removed the bandage from the left side where one of Pheng's bullets had creased his scalp. Since they'd had to cut away more of his hair to put in new stitches, he'd shaved the rest of his hair off. The change gave him an even more sinister look than before, but Cassiopia didn't look suitably alarmed.

"There's always the blond wig," she told him lightly.

"Why are you here?"

"I came to find out if I was a one-night stand after all."

He managed not to flinch. "What are you looking for, happily ever after?"

"Always."

Her hopeful expression was so open it took all his strength not to gather her in his arms.

"But I've discovered happily ever after is frustratingly elusive," she added.

Like her. She was a breath of spring sunshine on this crisp fall day while he stood there frozen like old man winter. How was it she could twist his insides like a pretzel? If things had been different…but they weren't.

"Maybe you keep looking in all the wrong places."

HE DIDN'T WANT HER. Cassy had begun to suspect as much but she would not let him see her cry. She'd known coming here like this was a risk. He wasn't ready to love or be loved and it was going to break her heart.

Her chin lifted in outward defiance. "So you're going to go back to hiding in the shadows again?"

She could see her question stung, as it was meant to.

They would tear each other apart at this rate, but she felt helpless to prevent it from happening.

"It's what I know best," he told her honestly.

"No. What you know best is how to create beauty out of clay." Why couldn't he see that? "Someday, maybe you'll accept that truth. Have a good life, Gabriel." She heard the pain threading her voice. "*I* intend to."

GABE WATCHED HER TURN and walk away with an ache that was physical.

You just going to let her go, pal?

It was as though Beacher stood beside him. He could hear his friend's mocking tone in his head.

You're pure magic when it comes to a ball of clay, but a real idiot when it comes to a woman.

"I don't know how to be what she needs."

Don't tell me, pal, tell her.

She'd reached her car and was opening the door. Her head was bowed in a way that reminded him of the first time he'd sent her away.

He was a fool, but he didn't want her to go.

"Cassiopia! Cassy! Wait!" He ran after her, more afraid now than he'd ever been in his life.

She swiped at her face before turning toward him. If she'd been crying, there was no sign of tears now.

"What did you call me?"

He paused, several feet from her. His chest felt as tight as if he'd run a marathon.

"That's the first time you've ever called me Cassy."

Gabe swallowed, wishing he didn't feel like an adolescent about to ask a girl out for the first time.

"I'm no good at personal stuff." Not anymore.

Maybe he never had been, but it had never been this important before. "Why would you want me?"

HIS VULNERABILITY struck her full force. Cassy fought an urge to fling herself against his chest and hold him tight. Instead, she worked to keep her voice even.

"That's certainly blunt and to the point. I'm a fool, I guess. I love you. I don't know why. You certainly don't deserve me."

She saw shock and more in his somber eyes. Was that hope?

"I know I don't. Cassiopia, I still don't remember what happened that day with your father. I get brief flashes, but I probably won't ever remember exactly what happened."

Relief left her knees week. "Is that what's bothering you? I thought we decided Carstairs sent you to the house for some reason."

"But I don't *know!* I'll never know for sure."

"So? I don't blame you for anything that happened. I wish I could take back my initial reaction, but I can't. I can only apologize."

He shook his head. "I'd have felt the same way in your place. You're like sunshine, Cassiopia—bright, open, giving. You said it yourself, I live in the shadows."

"You don't have to. Not anymore. Sun and shadows go together. See?"

SHE POINTED TO their mingled shadows on the sidewalk. Then she reached out to touch his scarred face. Gabe couldn't prevent a flinch as her soft fingers delicately traced the line of his scar.

"Each scar is a mark of honor and courage. You got this, and these—" she lightly touched the back of his hand "—trying to save my father. I believe that, even if you don't remember. You got this one—" her finger skimmed over his scalp near the spot Pheng's bullet had grazed "—saving me." Her eyes suddenly twinkled. "The one on the back of your head, however, is because you ride an idiot death machine, but I'll work on that one."

And he laughed. He couldn't help it. He loved this woman, every inch of her sassy, infuriating, gorgeous being.

"I love you."

The words sounded as rusty as they felt.

"It's about time you realized that."

He swooped her up then, kissing them both breathless.

"We're going to make a new start," she told him.

Warmed by what he saw in the depths of her eyes, he smiled back. "Right now?"

"Why not? I know where there's a room with a large bed. Of course, if you need to drive the rosebush to your friend Denny first…"

"I can be late. I'm told we artists are supposed to be eccentric and that would take too long."

"Hmm. We'll take it later then."

"Much later."

* * * * *

Don't miss Dani Sinclair's next Intrigue,
coming your way in February 2007!
Available wherever Harlequin Books are sold.

*Experience the anticipation, the thrill of the chase
and the sheer rush of falling in love!*

*Turn the page for a sneak preview of
a new book from Harlequin Romance
THE REBEL PRINCE
by Raye Morgan
On sale August 29th
wherever books are sold*

"Oh, no!"

The reaction slipped out before Emma Valentine could stop it, for there stood the very man she most wanted to avoid seeing again.

He didn't look any happier to see her.

"Well, come on, get on board," he said gruffly. "I won't bite." One eyebrow rose. "Though I might nibble a little," he added, mostly to amuse himself.

But she wasn't paying any attention to what he was saying. She was staring at him, taking in the royal blue uniform he was wearing, with gold braid and glistening badges decorating the sleeves, epaulettes and an upright collar. Ribbons and medals covered the breast of the short, fitted jacket. A gold-encrusted sabre hung at his side. And suddenly it was clear to her who this man really was.

She gulped wordlessly. Reaching out, he took her elbow and pulled her aboard. The doors slid closed. And finally she found her tongue.

"You…you're the prince."

He nodded, barely glancing at her. "Yes. Of course."

She raised a hand and covered her mouth for a moment. "I should have known."

"Of course you should have. I don't know why you didn't." He punched the ground-floor button to get the elevator moving again, then turned to look down at her. "A relatively bright five-year-old child would have tumbled to the truth right away."

Her shock faded as her indignation at his tone asserted itself. He might be the prince, but he was still just as annoying as he had been earlier that day.

"A relatively bright five-year-old child without a bump on the head from a badly thrown water polo ball, maybe," she said defensively. She wasn't feeling woozy any longer and she wasn't about to let him bully her, no matter how royal he was. "I was unconscious half the time."

"And just clueless the other half, I guess," he said, looking bemused.

The arrogance of the man was really galling.

"I suppose you think your 'royalness' is so obvious it sort of shimmers around you for all to see?" she challenged. "Or better yet, oozes from your pores like…like sweat on a hot day?"

"Something like that," he acknowledged calmly. "Most people tumble to it pretty quickly. In fact, it's hard to hide even when I want to avoid dealing with it."

"Poor baby," she said, still resenting his manner. "I guess that works better with injured people who are half asleep." Looking at him, she felt a strange emotion she couldn't identify. It was as though she wanted to prove something to him, but she wasn't sure what.

"And anyway, you know you did your best to fool me," she added.

His brows knit together as though he really didn't know what she was talking about. "I didn't do a thing."

"You told me your name was Monty."

"It is." He shrugged. "I have a lot of names. Some of them are too rude to be spoken to my face, I'm sure." He glanced at her sideways, his hand on the hilt of his sabre. "Perhaps you're contemplating one of those right now."

You bet I am.

That was what she would like to say. But it suddenly occurred to her that she was supposed to be working for this man. If she wanted to keep the job of coronation chef, maybe she'd better keep her opinions to herself. So she clamped her mouth shut, took a deep breath and looked away, trying hard to calm down.

The elevator ground to a halt and the doors slid open laboriously. She moved to step forward, hoping to make her escape, but his hand shot out again and caught her elbow.

"Wait a minute. *You're* a woman," he said, as though that thought had just presented itself to him.

"That's a rare ability for insight you have there, Your Highness," she snapped before she could stop herself. And then she winced. She was going to have to do better than that if she was going to keep this relationship on an even keel.

But he was ignoring her dig. Nodding, he stared at her with a speculative gleam in his golden eyes. "I've been looking for a woman, but you'll do."

She blanched, stiffening. "I'll do for what?"

He made a head gesture in a direction she knew was

opposite of where she was going and his grip tightened on her elbow.

"Come with me," he said abruptly, making it an order.

She dug in her heels, thinking fast. She didn't much like orders. "Wait! I can't. I have to get to the kitchen."

"Not yet. I need you."

"You what?" Her breathless gasp of surprise was soft, but she knew he'd heard it.

"I need you," he said firmly. "Oh, don't look so shocked. I'm not planning to throw you into the hay and have my way with you. I need you for something a bit more mundane than that."

She felt color rushing into her cheeks and she silently begged it to stop. Here she was, formless and stodgy in her chef's whites. No makeup, no stiletto heels. Hardly the picture of the femmes fatales he was undoubtedly used to. The likelihood that he would have any carnal interest in her was remote at best. To have him think she was hysterically defending her virtue was humiliating.

"Well, what if I don't want to go with you?" she said in hopes of deflecting his attention from her blush.

"Too bad."

"What?"

Amusement sparkled in his eyes. He was certainly enjoying this. And that only made her more determined to resist him.

"I'm the prince, remember? And we're in the castle. My orders take precedence. It's that old pesky divine rights thing."

Her jaw jutted out. Despite her embarrassment, she couldn't let that pass.

"Over my free will? Never!"

Exasperation filled his face.

"Hey, call out the historians. Someone will write a book about you and your courageous principles." His eyes glittered sardonically. "But in the meantime, Emma Valentine, you're coming with me."

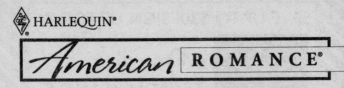

HARLEQUIN®

American ROMANCE®

IS PROUD TO PRESENT A GUEST APPEARANCE BY

QUILL
BOOK
AWARD
WINNING
AUTHOR

NEW YORK TIMES bestselling author
DEBBIE MACOMBER

The Wyoming Kid

The story of an ex–rodeo cowboy,
a schoolteacher and their journey to the altar.

"Best-selling Macomber, with more than
100 romances and women's fiction titles
to her credit, sure has a way of pleasing readers."
—*Booklist* on *Between Friends*

**The Wyoming Kid is available from
Harlequin American Romance in July 2006.**

If you enjoyed what you just read,
then we've got an offer you can't resist!

Take 2 bestselling love stories FREE!

Plus get a FREE surprise gift!